Best wishes

J

Angelo's Journey: From Bardi to Pontypridd

J. L. Harland

ISBN: 978-1-0686276-0-6

Editor: Linda Bradley

Cover design: Doug Harrett

Photograph: Mona Eendra on Unsplash

Contents

Acknowledgements

Angelo's Journey is set in the early 1970s when regular migration from Italy to Wales still took place. Although a work of fiction, we could never have written this story in such authentic detail without the input from Paula Servini (now Harrett). For example, one striking illustration was how Paula said her mother described leaving Italy as 'moving from colour to black and white as Wales was so dark and damp'. Paula gave us the finer details of what it was like to belong to the Italian migrant community in the 1970s, the social and religious occasions and the famous Italian cafe culture at the time.

We visited Prince's Restaurant in Pontypridd as part of our research. It still retains something of the old ways, a bit like stepping back in time, as one reviewer commented.

Thank you also to BBC Wales. We watched The Welsh Italians with Michela Chiappa which showed how the traditions are kept alive and how identities blend. Inner conflict caused by changing or blended identity and the idea of belonging/not belonging were themes we wanted to explore as Angelo moved between Bardi and Pontypridd.

As always, a huge thanks to our writing groups, Writers Enjoying Words and Criminal Fairies, and family and friends. We couldn't do it without your support.

Finally, grateful thanks to our readers who reviewed our first novel, What Lies Between Them, to which Angelo's Journey is a prequel. We didn't realise when we started out how important reviews are to visibility of a novel. When you have read Angelo's Journey please consider leaving an honest review on Amazon. Thank you.

To Bridget – superfan!

Bardi, Italy. Early 1970s.

Papa

'Angelo. *Alzati velocemente.*' Get up quick.

Mamma's talking but I struggle to understand as I drag myself from sleep.

'Your Papa's not come home,' she says. She's out of breath climbing up to my bedroom in the eaves and stands by the door, hands over her heart.

I sigh, get dressed and start to look for him. He's probably been on one of his drinking binges. The outhouse first. I've found him sleeping it off there before, although he claimed he was fixing something. But there's no sign, so I walk out to the fields.

It's a perfect April day, the sun coming up and the dew rising from the grass. The air smells of Spring, loud with birdsong. The castle at Bardi is in the distance, still misty as if in soft focus with its tumble of red-tiled houses below. Somewhere a bell rings across the valley. Far below the river Ceno winds its way. It's going to be a warm day.

I find him lying peacefully, as though resting, in the top field. Curled on one side, his stick fallen beside him. Not moving. Not breathing. I check his pulse. Nothing. I feel panic rise in me. How do I tell Mamma?

Looking at him lying on the grass like that with his eyes closed, he seems peaceful. Quiet and still. But already the flies are buzzing around, and I need to do something.

I've seen plenty of dead creatures; death from old age, disease, being attacked by a fox or a bird of prey. You pick them up if you can. You bury them. But with Papa I don't know what to do. I can't tell Mamma until I know what's happening. It seems wrong to lift his body, so I run back the way I've come and out through the yard towards Uncle Carlo's farm, further along the track up the mountainside. A viper darts in front of me and then disappears again. The geese hiss at me as I approach, and a cat scurries away behind a hedge. I hoped to find Uncle Carlo outside by the pump or in the barn but he's in the kitchen. The smell of cattle seems to follow me indoors, pungent but not unpleasant. Familiar. Uncle Carlo is calm when I explain, hitches the trailer up to the tractor and we go together to collect Papa.

Since then, things are a blur. The doctor comes and examines the body.

'A massive heart attack,' he says, 'brought on by everything he experienced during the war and made worse by the drinking. I did warn him.'

Aunt Violetta and Mamma sit crying and talking and crying again. We've so many visitors. Bad news travels quickly. Father Bernardo calls to make funeral arrangements. A Requiem Mass is arranged. I'm not sure it's what Papa would have wanted. Too much fuss; but Violetta insists.

What am I going to do with my dreams of leaving, finding my way in the world, starting a business, making money? If it wasn't for Mamma, I might have gone already. And how is she going to manage now? I expect I could work the farm if I had to. But I don't know if that's what I want to do with my life. Then again, do I have any choice?

Uncle Carlo tells me about Papa when he was a young man.

‘Enrico was fearless. He was always playing tricks and getting into mischief. We used to swim in the Ceno. He’d jump off the rocks, yelling and shouting. Showing off, of course. He was forever teasing and flirting with the girls. I think that’s why your Mamma fell for him. He was different then. A big brother to look up to.’

Uncle Carlo’s a large man, florid cheeks and narrow dark eyes, like a hawk. A younger version of Papa. He wasn’t old enough to fight in the war, but he remembers how altered his brother was after coming home. He tells me, ‘War changes a man. When your Papa went off to fight, he was full of excitement, a boy, but when he came back…he’d aged by ten or fifteen years.’

He comes over to me and puts his arm across my shoulder. ‘You’re the head of the household now. It’s your sacred duty to look after your mother.’

I long to travel, have adventures, learn a new skill, earn money. But I know Uncle Carlo is right. I must stay and look after Mamma. I wish I’d a brother or sister, or that Mamma and Papa were not almost into middle age when they had me. I’ve been too busy shouldering the workload to grieve, but my heart is thick as treacle. Mamma sits in her chair by the empty fireplace with a handkerchief wet and scrunched up in her hand, her eyes heavy and swollen from tears, rocking backwards and forwards.

This is the worst day of my life.

Funeral

We Italians take death seriously. *Il rispetto*. Respect for the dead. I keep vigil beside the body all night. The coffin sits on the dining table. I stare at the mottled mirror on the wall and set of faded photographs. The fireplace is empty and, as I watch, a spider makes his web in one corner. I look around the room. The candles are almost out, spreading eerie shadows on the wall.

I swallow the lump in my throat as daylight comes into the room. It's hard to see this body, so still, and think of it as my father. His skin looks waxy and already the body is starting to decompose. Even the flowers and burning candles can't disguise the smell in this airless room.

Today is Papa's funeral. The cockerel is crowing outside and the sound seems like an invasion. In here is death; outside, life continues.

The daily routine of the farm begins. Feeding the animals, milking the goats, checking that everything is the way it should be. The hearse will arrive at eleven o'clock to take us to Chiesa di Santa Maria Addolorato, the big church in Piazza Vittoria. I worry about the cost.

I know we're poor, although I haven't seen the accounts yet. Scratching a living. Mamma's sweaters are darned over and over again.

The sun is high in the sky and I can feel sweat trickling down my face and neck on the slow walk behind the hearse along the winding roads, up and down, from the farm to the town. Insects buzz and swifts dart high in the sky. Butterflies flit from flower to flower and the scent of rosemary, grass and sweet mountain air is all around. People join us as we walk, all dressed in black. Next to me, Mamma's gown rustles. I think it must belong to Aunt Violetta as I've never seen it before. It seems to take forever before the front of the church looms up before us. The shops are open and seeing the butcher's with its carcasses, tongues lolling out, makes me feel nauseous, thinking of the body ahead of us in the coffin. Even today with a funeral procession the Vespas zip around and the droning reverberates in my head.

Blessed coolness inside the church. Everything feels unreal. Our steps echo as we make our way down the aisle. I'm reminded of the holiness of this place by the solemnity of the priest's chanting. We enter, dip our fingers in the holy water, kneel and make the sign of the cross. Mamma's knees are stiff, and I place a hand under her elbow to help her up. She gives me a tearful smile through her veil.

High above the altar I look up and see the figure of Jesus gazing down. I wonder if God is watching and what future he has in mind for me. The Requiem Mass continues, the priest's voice murmuring, the mourners' responses. Incense fills the air, making my eyes water and my throat itch. It feels like hours before we can leave the church and follow the hearse again towards the cemetery. My shirt chafes my neck and the sun beats down on us, burning my tired eyes. I hold Mamma's arm as we walk, and she stumbles a few times. I'm glad when it's over, and Papa is buried.

Afterwards, many come back to the house. The men are outside smoking, and the women are in the kitchen, preparing food. I feel as if I can still taste the smell of death in my mouth. I long for my bed under the eaves to escape – to dream. Uncle Carlo offers me a cigarette and I take it, being careful to follow how he holds it. I inhale the smoke and immediately start to cough. He claps me on the back.

'Not a habit then,' he says, laughing at my discomfort. Then all serious again, he says, 'You know the farm is your responsibility now, Angelo. How will you manage?' I shake my head. I don't know.

I've no answer, only questions.

Debts

I'm just in from the field, washed and changed out of my work clothes, when we have an unexpected visitor. It's baking hot out on the hill and my muscles ache everywhere from all the work. More than a month now since Papa passed away and there is never a quiet time on the farm, always jobs to do. I boasted to myself that I could run the farm, but I have to face it, it's too hard. What with looking after the animals, the crops, going to market, keeping our plot of vegetables going, it's a massive task. There was enough to keep two men working all the hours God sends. But on my own, even with some help from Uncle Carlo, it seems I'm at the bottom of an enormous mountain that I have to climb, creeping inch by inch, alone, up many steep and slippery slopes. And, in my heart of hearts, I know I don't want to undertake this journey. But I don't tell anyone, least of all Mamma.

We're surprised when there's a knock on the door. Mamma tells me to open it and there is Signora Barbieri. She smells of perfume and cigarettes and her eyes flash at me. Stabbing her cigarette out on the pointed toe of her high heels, with her blonde hair tied back and her sunglasses perched on her head, she looks me up and down and smiles.

'Well, well, so you're Enrico's boy. All grown-up.'

I hear Mamma put a plate down sharply on the table and come to stand behind me.

'Loretta,' she says. 'Please come in.'

Signora Barbieri strolls in and I wonder what this is all about. I know she and her brothers have a business in Parma and they're distant relatives of Papa's on his mother's side. Surely, though, she hasn't come to pay her respects so late? She wasn't at the funeral, I'm certain of that, despite the crowd attending. Someone like her would stand out.

Loretta waves away Mamma's offer of a drink and sits down at the table, crossing one slim leg over the other. Sunshine sparkles from the diamonds on her hand.

'A very handsome boy. You are lucky, Matilda. Pity you only had the one.'

I feel Mamma's anger in the way she sits up straighter in her chair. Something's going on between them I don't understand. I feel uncomfortable, belittled, when Signora Barbieri comes close and pinches my cheek. She's the opposite of Mamma, razor-sharp, polished and sophisticated. No black cardigan buttoned to the neck for her.

'And how are you coping?' the Signora asks Mamma.

'Times are hard, as you know, with the economic situation, but we have help from Carlo and my sister Violetta.' I can see Mamma isn't going to tell Signora Barbieri the truth about our situation.

'Good. Then I'll come straight to the point. About the debts.'

The debts. What was she talking about?

'Sadly, the grace time is now over, and we need repayment. Enrico has fallen behind for months and things are serious.'

'But…' Mamma's worn hands, swollen with the arthritis, twist in the drying cloth she's holding. 'No. That can't be right. He's been paying you back regularly.'

Signora Barbieri coughs, a delicate and affected sound, and her husky smoker's voice answers, 'Well, he might have told you that. Unfortunately, this is not the case. I'm paying a friendly visit to talk things through, to see what can be done so that we don't have to . . . make things more formal.'

I feel my head whirling. We've very little money, but I thought we were just about getting by. What's all this? Debts. How much and why?

'So, you'll need to get some money to us straightaway, let's say 150,000 lire to start, and, because you're family, we're willing to wait for the rest – we won't press you like we would others.' Her smile holds no warmth.

It turns out that there's a loan secured against the farm. We owe the Barbieri family large sums.

'Last year, with the market, well…' Mamma waves her hands in the air as if that helps to explain. 'Enrico couldn't sell enough to cover the costs of running the farm. Animals still needed to be fed. The price of foodstuffs had gone up as well as his profits going down. But I didn't know he hadn't been paying it back.' She utters a choked sob. 'And I wondered how he had money for his drinking.' I hate to see her like this. Even after death, it seems Papa causes her to suffer.

Later, I look out of the window down the valley, a beautiful scene, much loved by visitors and walkers. I can see its beauty, but all that nature doesn't stop me wanting to leave, to earn a better life for myself. What am I going to do?

Mamma's gone to visit Aunt Violetta to ask if she will lend us the 150,000 lire. More debt. What a nightmare this summer is turning out to be. I don't blame Papa. Not really. Uncle Carlo has explained how war changed him. The alcohol was Papa's way of dealing with his demons.

A knock on the door again. But this time it's Giuseppe.

'Hey, *amico*. I've come to take you out for a swim in the river.'

I look at his face. Happy, healthy. My best friend from school. A lifetime ago. He's back from the UK, visiting family there. He missed the funeral but now gives me a bear hug and pats my back. It brings tears to my eyes. He doesn't need to tell me he's sorry about Papa and this awful situation. He understands.

'I should…'

'No.' Giuseppe delivers his killer line. 'I saw your mother on her way to your Aunt Violetta's house and she told me to take you out.'

We walk down the lane, keeping to the shade where possible in the fierce midday heat, and head towards the river. Someone has a radio playing and I hear *Grande Grande Grande* whisper through the air as we pass a house. In the town life is as usual. Little Fiats toot, weaving through the narrow streets near the old quarter. The summer visitors have begun to arrive; we hear a babble of English, French and German.

The bustle fades as we near the river. Giuseppe flops down on the grass and we watch the dragonflies for a while before he speaks.

'So, you're going to stay and look after the farm, or not? What are your plans?'

'It's complicated.'

'I know. You wanted to go out into the world, on your adventures.'

I kick a stone and a cloud of dust flurries upwards off the baked-dry road.

'No chance. Papa's put paid to that, in more ways than one. And I thought it was Mamma who'd stop me.'

On the way to the river, I tell Giuseppe about Signora Barbieri's visit and the debts.

'Them?' Giuseppe spits on the ground. 'The trouble they've caused – and the brothers, you've seen them, they're nasty.'

He's right. You don't get on the wrong side of the Barbieri family.

'Trouble is there are too many people needing money and that lot, sitting pretty, ready to lend it and screw you over with high interest rates.'

I can see Giuseppe is starting on one of his political rants about capitalism and socialism. After everything I've been through over the last two months, it feels good, a relief to hear him talking his big ideas. We swim and after, we dry ourselves in the sun and talk, leaving our clothes to dry on the stone slabs.

'Did you enjoy your visit to South Wales?'

Giuseppe shrugs. 'It was all right. Too wet for me. Imagine, in June, *amico*, wearing jumpers and coats. It's a strange place. People gossiping, like here.' He grinned.

'There are a lot of people from Bardi, but it doesn't feel like home.'

It's time for me to get back. I need to milk the goats and start to clear some land for autumn planting. It will be hard to dig as it's overgrown and the earth dry and cracked. We part at the crossroads but not before Giuseppe gives me another friendly hug.

'*Morto un papa, la vita continua.* Life goes on. You'll be fine, Angelo. Just you wait and see.'

I wish I could believe that.

Father Bernardo visits

Our worries increase as each day passes. I'm so weary from trying to work on the land all day. In the night, I look again and again at the bills, hoping that, as if by some miracle, my calculations are wrong. Hopeless. My eyes itch and my body aches but there is no respite. Mamma is determined to hold on to the land. I've tried to reason with her; sadly, it's useless.

'The land's important. It's your birth right. When we thought I was barren it would have passed to your uncle and his family. Thanks be to God I delivered you, a boy, to carry the name and own the land your Papa toiled for.' She crosses herself and gazes upwards towards heaven.

'But Mamma. I'm not a farmer, you know that. I like being outdoors in the summer but it's hard in the winter. And we've so many debts. How can we pay them all? We've got nothing to sell. The cow has gone. We need the goats for milk and cheese. All we have left to sell is a couple of stony fields. The rabbits are running wild and I don't know what to do next. The Barbieri boys won't wait too long for their money. *Trovarsi fra l'incudine e il Martello,'* We are between the anvil and the hammer.

'God will provide. He'll send us an answer.'

I roll my eyes as she crosses herself again. What does she really think? Does she mourn Papa at all? It's his fault we're in this mess. Mamma looks so ancient now. It's as though she has aged tenfold overnight, bent and frail. Her skin is wrinkled like paper. Her eyes sad and empty. She's not eating. I know. I watch her at supper time. It must be grief. We don't even have enough flour for her to bake every day and no money to buy more.

The hens are laying so I have an egg for breakfast mid-morning. Although we have vegetables growing and we can forage for porcini and other mushrooms there never seems to be enough to fill my appetite. Hunger is my constant companion. I try to eat more slowly and pretend I'm not hungry so that Mamma will sit with me and take some nourishment. But she shakes her head, tells me she's already eaten and drinks some water. It gurgles in her empty belly.

Every day she treks down to church to pray. It would be better if she helped with the weeding. Her herb garden is becoming overgrown, but her eyes are blinded by religion. I've lost hope in God intervening and providing us with the means to carry on living here. I don't go to mass on Sunday. There's no time. It's just another day to work in life's constant struggle.

Then, Mamma comes back from the town and Father Bernardo's with her. I see them from the field where I'm working. He's taller than Mamma and walks with a slight limp. His cassock is stretched over his rounded belly, the hem of it raising a cloud of dust with each step. I suppose he's going to nag me about not attending mass. I'll keep my temper for Mamma's sake. I won't ask him if he's come to work in the fields with me. That would be more help than preaching. Mamma beckons and her voice drifts across the warm air. She sounds almost cheerful.

'Angelo, come in a moment. Have a glass of water and sit with Father Bernardo.'

Once, it would have been a coffee or even a glass of wine for the good father. See what we are reduced to now. Mamma would take the priest into the parlour, but

I'm wearing my work clothes. Too dusty for the best room. We go into the kitchen instead. It's in deep shade, the shutters closed to keep the room cool. A fly buzzes around the ceiling. There's a lingering smell of garlic.

I take off my cap and wipe the sweat from my brow. Run my hand over my trousers before the priest grasps my calloused palm in his two soft ones, as if I'm a long-lost relative. His eyes seem to bore through me, searching for the answer to a question he hasn't asked yet.

'Father,' I say, nodding. I wait. What's he doing here? What does he want?

'We haven't seen you at mass since the funeral. It's been months now. Are you well?'

'Yes, father. I'm quite well. Thank you.'

We both wait. Mamma puts the cups of water on the table and I sit. Father Bernardo has already taken Papa's chair at the head of the table. For some reason, I feel resentful. I can't explain why. I should try to make conversation but still I say nothing. Silence hangs, like a threat, in the air. At last Mamma can wait no longer.

'I've been talking to Father Bernardo about our problems.'

'Everyone knows our problems. I thought you'd been talking to God about them.' I hear the edge of sarcasm in my voice and feel a flash of shame. I shouldn't take out my frustrations on Mamma. It's just as difficult for her. Maybe more so as she has to go into town and pretend not to hear the whispers. I blush.

To my surprise Father Bernardo laughs. 'Oh indeed. Signora Fiorelli has been asking God but also me. Perhaps a more practical solution.'

I'm not sure how to react. Was that a joke? Should I laugh too? I glance at Mamma and she's wringing her hands. Something has been said. Something has been decided. Surely Mamma doesn't expect me to go to the priesthood? As these thoughts run through my head, Mamma lays a hand on my shoulder.

'Father Bernardo knows people who've had money problems.' She hesitates and, even in the dim light, I notice her eyes are filled with tears. 'He may have a solution. A way to help.' My heart beats faster. What's this solution? The fly lands on the table beside my glass. I want to pummel it with my fist but restrain myself.

'Yes,' the priest says and clears his throat a little before continuing. 'My flock is spread far and wide, not only here but also abroad. We've had people travelling from Bardi to Wales in search of work. I have been there sometimes to visit. Your friend, Giuseppe, has family there, I know.' I nod, unsure where this conversation is leading. He exchanges glances with Mamma. 'There are opportunities. Work. In the mines, not so much now. But the factories. In the cafés. Some people have made great successes selling gelato. This isn't new. We've second generations of families who come back to visit. You will have seen them, heard them in the town. You could have a fine life there.'

It's as if he's prepared the speech. He looks into my eyes and then at Mamma. I'm frowning. I don't understand. Why would Mamma want to move away from the farm? All the time she's going on about my legacy and how important the land is to us, to Papa's memory. Now – a move to Wales?

'But … the farm?'

Then, it's Mamma's turn. 'Your cousin Francesco could rent the farm from us. He's got a feel for the land and three strong boys to help. Uncle Carlo has already asked if we would consider it.'

‘I’m confused. What exactly have you been doing? What do you expect me to do?’ Panic is rising in me. ‘Are you saying we’re to move to Wales? How’s that going to pay the debts?’

I’m angry now. Angry with Papa for dying and leaving us this millstone to carry. Angry with Mamma for talking behind my back. Angry with the priest for suggesting this idea. Angry with the world.

Mamma moves away and I hear a sob. Father Bernardo takes control. His voice is deep, measured. He rests a hand on my arm.

‘I’ve not explained properly. I’m sorry. Forgive me, my son. We should have involved you in our discussions. I have heard, through my contacts in Wales, of a business that needs a young man, willing to work hard. The owners are from Bardi. They run a café in a town called Pontypridd. It’s in a valley, so, like… a little like the countryside here. There are mountains and the people are friendly. There’s a small Italian community, well established, so you wouldn’t feel isolated. Best of all, you’d be able to send money home to your mother to pay off the debts.’

He beams at me as if my feelings don't matter. It seems as though things have been decided. I'm to go away, alone, to a strange land.

'And Mamma?'

The priest shakes his head. 'If your cousin rents the farm your mother can afford to stay with her sister, Violetta, and pay off some of the debt. With the money you'll be able to send back as well, within a couple of years you should be able to return to Bardi and the farm. If God is willing and things work out. It's a great opportunity, *ragazzo mio.*'

My head is reeling. I never wanted to be a farmer – but this? Travel. A chance to see a bit of the world. My dream. But work in a land where I don't know the language. The culture. The customs. That's not what I expected. I take a deep breath.

As if sensing my mood, Father Bernardo gets to his feet. 'You need to think about this, Angelo. It may not be what you want. But…' he looks at me with meaning in his eyes, 'you need to pay your debts. This way you can keep the farm, which is what your Mamma wants, and gain back your family honour. We'll talk again when you've had time to think about it all.'

He nods at Mamma. '*Buongiorno*, Signora Fiorelli.'

I'm too shocked to move for a moment. I look at Mamma and see her distress. She's as uncertain about the idea as I am. She shakes her head, holds out her hands, palms upwards.

'I asked God. It's the only way.'

So, my fate is sealed. I'm to go to Wales.

Leaving Bardi

As if she's read my earlier thoughts, Mamma goes out after Father Bernardo has left to start weeding the herb garden and vegetable plot to the side of the house. She's wearing the straw hat she's had for so many years, the edges frayed and ragged. Makes my heart break. I know she can't labour like this. It's too much for her. My mood changes in a flash, to a rainbow of exciting ideas; away from the fierce anger I felt at having decisions made on my behalf, without any discussion. I'm proud of my strength and youth. I can earn money to help us; I feel a surge of excitement at the challenge. I know I'm capable of succeeding in this new life, despite the niggling doubts about moving so far away and guilt at leaving Mamma and the farm, my inheritance. But two things are uppermost in my mind as I walk out to talk to Mamma. This is the opportunity I dreamt of and I know I can make it work.

Mamma straightens up slowly and leans on the handle of her hoe.

'We'll have a bean stew tonight. I found enough at the end of that row there, though it's covered in weeds. *Tutta fa brodo*.'

She doesn't look at me, but out across the valley.

'You're happy to go and live with Aunt Violetta?'

That makes her turn back to me.

'*Mimmo*, I know you want to leave the valley and go out into the world. I was dreading it. But life changes so suddenly. We lost Papa and God has decided this is how it will be. I didn't expect it so soon or in this way, but I pray it'll be the right thing for you and for me.'

I hug her. I don't have her solid faith, but I hope she's right.

'So, now we just have the arrangements to make,' Mamma says through her tears.

Some weeks later

The storm last night was fierce with the wind howling round the roof and the rain lashing down. Summer storms with flashes of lightning across the valley and thunderclaps echoing round the mountains. We knew it was forecast and I'd make sure the outhouse door was tightly shut – it's started to come off its hinges – and the animals were safely inside. But now, as I come out of my bedroom to start my jobs, I see that the roof is leaking, in the corner under the eaves. The dark stain on the ceiling and the beading of rainwater is a new worry. I hope it's not an omen that I should stay.

I tell Mamma and she says I must ask Uncle Carlo to help fix it before I leave. One more in a whole list of jobs to do. Now it's settled I'm going away, we've started arguing again. She wants to fuss about where I will stay when I get to Wales; how we will keep in touch; which families we know; whose relatives are there already.

'I'll be fine, Mamma.'

Father Bernardo visits often. He's a kind man and I'm surprised how much he seems to know about the ways of the world, despite being a priest. He tells me it will take two days to get to Pontypridd, a long journey by train, boat and bus. He's been teaching me some English to add to what little I learnt in school; and he says there's another language spoken in that valley, like we have our own dialect here in Bardi, French words mingling with the Italian.

'It will be very different, Angelo. You must learn to be patient. That's hard for a young man, I know. But all will turn out well in the end. You'll see.' He smiles at me and nods encouragement. I've been going to mass again, which I think pleases him and Mama. 'You'll get used to the new life there. The work will be quite unlike farm work. A change of direction for you.'

But that's what excites me. I love the idea that it's different. Here I know everybody; every street and shop; every sound and smell. I could walk from the farm to the cobbled streets of the castle blindfold.

My cousin Francesco's been over to discuss the arrangements. He's renting out his place, which is even smaller than ours, and will move into the house and work the land with his wife and boys. That's good. He'll look after the repairs. He's older than me, very serious, talking about agriculture and crop rotation. He went to college and has a lot of theory behind him. Uncle Carlo laughs at him a little, but Mamma seems happy with the situation and says he's a sensible man. As for where she will live, she was always closest to Violetta and that house is big enough for her to have a good-sized room, pay her way, and a little of the debt with the money we'll get from Francesco. He's promised more if he has a high yield harvest in the summer.

I'm on my way to town to buy a few items for repairing the roof. Uncle Carlo gave me the money, clapping me on the back and saying, 'See it as my leaving gift to you. We can't have the old house going to rack and ruin.'

He's so different from Papa in temperament. But maybe it was the war, as Uncle Carlo says. Mamma must have loved Papa to marry him, but I never saw much happiness or affection between them. Sad to think of, now Papa's gone.

I start wondering what the girls are like in Wales and not really noticing where I'm walking, but ahead of me, coming in my direction, I see Signor Barbieri. He looks a bit like his sister, tall, same blonde hair, although fat as well, as though a balloon has blown him up from the inside. He's very broad and strong, along with being heavy, and he's smiling at me now, stopping to chat.

'*Buongiorno*, Angelo Fiorelli. My sister tells me we're all in order and you're going away to Wales to earn your fortune.'

He comes too close, his stomach leading, almost touching me. 'Plenty of money to be made. A fine young man like you, too. Lots of opportunities.'

His small blue eyes look intent, his breath foul on my cheek.

'Your poor Mamma. Losing her husband and now you.'

I'm not sure what the threat is, but I can feel it. Thank goodness Mamma is staying with Aunt Violetta.

'Two years remember. Two years.' And he laughs as though this is a joke. That's the time they have given us to clear the debt, with interest, of course.

The encounter leaves a nasty taste in my mouth. I'll have to make sure I succeed in my new life and pay the money back. No one in our close family has the sort of wealth to repay it in one go. And they mean business, this Barbieri family. They may be distant relatives of Papa's, but I wouldn't trust them an inch. Why did Papa take out such a large loan with them? Was he drunk at the time? Or was it something else? A mystery and I doubt we'll ever know now.

I'm due to leave at the beginning of September, only a couple of weeks away. The house is getting emptier and emptier as we sell furniture to give some money to Aunt Violetta for the funeral. I hadn't realised but some of it had a value – furniture and linens my mother brought with her when she married. Mamma says she'd prefer to have the money now, so that we clear our debts as soon as we can. And, anyway, Francesco's wife is from Parma and has her own ideas of what she wants in the house.

I paint the ceiling where the leak has stained it and help Mamma sort the items she wants to take with her. There's an oil colour of the castle painted by one of her uncles and she has some favourite china. She still seems in shock, frail, not sturdy like she was before Papa died.

One of my last jobs is to go into the parlour and pull out the chest again, which has all the papers Papa stored there on the business of the farm. He told me often enough that the farm was my inheritance and I should work for it, but he never showed me much about the business side. I was just an extra pair of hands, a labourer at his beck and call, even though I've a good head for figures and could often work out profit and loss as well, or better, than him when we went to market. Maybe if he'd shared more of the farm management, I'd have more interest in taking over one day. But the more I find out about his financial affairs now, the more I realise why he didn't want to share any of it with me, or Mamma. It was a mess.

The room is quiet and any sound echoes, now there's so little furniture in it. There's a hint of autumn and the leaves on the tree outside the window, curled and dry, tap against the pane. I sigh. That's another job – to cut the branches back. I may get around to it before I go. First, I must finish sorting the contents of the box. I glance at the table, remembering where the coffin lay only four months ago. Everything has changed since then.

I take out a pile of papers ready to burn and, when there's little left in the box, I feel a sudden lump in my throat seeing, at the bottom, a small red notebook, with Papa's spidery handwriting: pages full of notes, his plans to buy new livestock and rebuild the barn and outhouse and I see why Papa took out the large loan.

All for nothing. He drank away his dreams and I, his only son, am leaving the farm with a halter of debt round my neck.

Will I ever come back to put things right?

Pontypridd, Wales.

Arrival

Homesickness gnaws at my gut like the rats used to chew the sacks of wheat in the barn. If I was hungry, I could eat to ease the pain, but this is much deeper. An aching. A longing that can't be satisfied. I tell myself I'm lucky. I don't work underground, like the miners who come into the café or spend long hours on a factory line. But – it doesn't help. At home there were friends I could talk to, neighbours, the priest, Mamma. Here I feel so alone. Still a stranger, despite the community of Italians who've made their home here. I didn't expect this terrible feeling before I left home, dreaming of adventures out in the world.

When I walk the narrow streets of Pontypridd on my way to work, I think of the mountains around Bardi and the castle standing tall; a landmark for miles. My jacket doesn't keep out the dampness and I have to wrap my arms around myself for warmth. A low mist hangs over the hills, shrouding them. It feels eerie, muffling some of the sounds, like the traffic. When I arrived here in October, summer was over, but it was still pleasant. Now, at the end of November, everything looks different.

The light and colour of Italy is missing. Even in winter we would have days when the sky was bright and spun a sheen of silver over the land. I miss our blue skies, the terracotta roof tops, green fields and trees and how in summer the white-hot sun reflected on the windows of the houses. I miss my old life so much it hurts.

Here, everything is shades of grey – pewter, slate, charcoal, lead – and slag heaps dominate the landscape of these valley towns and villages. The coal industry is in decline, but its ugliness is all around. The air itself seems grey with smoke from the coal fires and the cigarettes. That cigarette Uncle Carlo gave me at the funeral was the only time I tried to smoke. I'm glad I didn't develop the habit. I don't like it and I can't afford it. My clothes reek of food and cigarettes from the café and I'm sure the smell clings to my hair and skin. I can wash my hair in the mornings in the basin, but my landlady only permits one bath a week. Saturday night.

When the café closes on that day, I go back to Signora Rossi's house and have my bath. I've fallen asleep more than once in the bliss of that warm water.

The rain is one of the things I hate most about this place. It seems to be like that all the time. Sometimes it's a relentless battering drumming on the rooftops and bouncing off the ground. Other days, like today, it's silent, hardly seen, drenching hair, face and clothing with a fine layer of moisture.

The miners come to the café from work with their blackened faces and hands. Scars heal with coal trapped in the skin, so they never look truly clean. Their hands are calloused, like my father's, and mine too when I worked with the earth on the farm. Stefano says when he came here many years ago mining was the work for most of the men and that the coal dust seemed to fill the air. But the mines are closing and the men, and women, are finding work in the factories.

As for me, my hands are red and chapped. Soft palmed, like a girl's, from all the water. I seem to spend most of my days washing. Dishes, floors, tables, toilet. Then there's the food preparation. Peeling potatoes and other vegetables. This isn't the life I thought I was going to have. Already I'm sad and disillusioned but I mustn't tell Mamma how unhappy I am in this place with people who speak in strange ways. It's only been a few weeks and I know I must give it time. Tonight, I'll write to Mamma again. I'll tell her about my room with Signora Rossi. She mustn't worry about me. She has enough problems, living as a lodger without a kitchen of her own. Her brother-in-law, Violetta's husband, is a good man but he can be forthright and difficult at times. I hope she's settled there.

Pontypridd,
December
1972

Dear Mamma,

I hope you are looking after yourself and not worrying about me too much. I'm settling here in Ponty. That's what the local people call it. It's a good-sized town. There's a big store in the market square called the Co-Op and many more shops on a street named after the local river, Taff Street.

Although a lot of things are new and strange, there are many similarities between this town and Bardi. I'm sure you'd like the market on Wednesdays and Saturdays. It stretches over two streets and whole place is buzzing then. You can hardly move. There's one seller who does tricks with crockery, shouting out sales talk so fast I can't understand a word, but people stop to watch, like a show. I think you could buy almost anything here. There's an indoor market too where they have butchers, a greengrocer and lots of other stalls. And a haberdashery that you'd love with wool for knitting, pretty fabric and bright ribbons and buttons. Are you still sewing? Is Aunt Violetta keeping you busy? How do you spend your time now you don't have to look after the house, garden and animals on the farm?

It's busy in the café too and Stefano makes me work very hard. But I think of what Papa used to say about hard work not hurting anyone and keep my head down, learning these new skills. My English isn't good enough to talk much to the customers, so I do the cleaning and preparation. I appreciate now how hard you worked in making our meals and keeping house.

My landlady, Signora Rossi, is a good cook so, between the leftovers at the café and her cooking, I fear I may become too fat. She makes her own pasta and sauces, but it's difficult to get ripe tomatoes here at this time of the year, so I think she uses cans. The smell of onions laced with garlic is wafting up the stairs to my room as I write this. My mouth is watering and stomach growling. She sings as she cooks too. Familiar songs from home and I've heard that at Easter there are dances and they bring over bands. That will be a big party.

I sleep in Signora Rossi's daughter Olivia's room while she's away. She's going to be a teacher and has lodgings in Cardiff where she's studying. It's a small room but then the whole house is small and perched on the side of a mountain, squeezed together with others like a pack of cards. I have a bed and a box to keep my clothes. Signora Rossi does my washing as well as feeding me so you don't need to worry.

I hope the money I'm sending you is a help. I pray that we can pay off all Papa's debts and gain our good name again. I think of you every day and wish I could be with you this Christmas, but it's impossible. Stefano has already told me I'm expected to work every day, except Christmas Day when everyone will go to mass. After the first three months I am allowed one day off a month. But I can't complain. I've a roof over my head, clothes on my back and food in my belly.

I shall pray for you on Sunday and light a candle on Christmas Day at mass. Father Bernardo will be glad to know I go to mass when I can.

Your loving son,

Angelo

My heart's so heavy I think it'll break. Sheer fatigue stops me from protesting too much about the work. But how much worse it must be for Mamma. Living with Aunt Violetta and her family must be terrible for a proud woman like her, accepting charity; even though she's paying some rent for her room. Mamma's lost her husband, son, home and dignity in one fell swoop of death's wing. How can she bear it?

I must try to be more optimistic and look to the future. Advent is around the corner. and there's a sense of the festivities to come. Children are getting excited and, in the cafe, despite some of them screaming and having tantrums, Stefano welcomes them with open arms. It's all good business. The women like it here and come most mornings, sitting for an hour or so, gossiping over their coffee, about family and the latest chances of jobs at one of the factories. On market days the café is packed, and Stefano is happy as he sees the money rolling into the till.

Signora Rossi tells me Olivia will be home for a month at Christmas, so I'll have to sleep on the sofa downstairs during that time. I don't mind. Olivia was here when I first arrived, preparing to go to teacher training college in Cardiff – the capital city. It's only a few miles away but it might as well be the moon. Olivia promised she'll help me improve my English when she's home. She's very clever, and pretty too, so I look forward to that. She told me that's she's happy for me to stay in her room while she's away as her Mamma, Signora Rossi, a widow, wants someone in the house to keep her company. As for Signora Rossi, I think my company is poor as I'm so tired, but her smile, when I drag myself home from work, is always warm and welcoming. Her older girl, Sophia, is away, married and living in the next valley and, with Olivia in Cardiff, the money I pay her as rent helps ease things for the family.

I say an Ave Maria every night and hope the Virgin listens to me and will soothe this pain in my heart.

Work in the café

As I walk from my digs in Vaughan Street to the café, I'm getting acclimatised to the air, the look of the place and even beginning to find my way around. Ponty is a town with lots of streets and some are so narrow and steep it is hard to see how cars manage the roads. I have noticed the chapels, as they are called, too, so different from our big church in Piazza Vittoria at home. They are large, no towers, stone built, with slate roofs. The Catholic Church, which Signora Rossi showed me, is called St Dyfrig's, not far away in Treforest.

Father Bernardo was right to warn me that everything would be different. But how could I have imagined what it would really be like? So many people packed in close together, like Bardi with its flats and houses in the centre of town, but also different somehow. The buildings here are made for wind, cold and rain. I can't explain. The difference is everything altogether, the people, the culture and language, the houses, shops and streets.

Ponty's a busy centre for the whole valley. Sometimes, like now when I'm walking to the café, people nod to me. Other times schoolkids run after me shouting words I don't understand. I'm glad I began to learn English before I arrived, or I'd find it even more difficult to adjust.

The work is every bit as tough as it was on the farm and Stefano is a hard task master. At the start, when he found out how badly I was peeling potatoes, he hit me, told me I was wasting half the potato. If I prepared the next one like that, he would take money out of my wages. But at least the café is warm and the smell of the espresso machine reminds me of the café at home. This big adventure starting a new life for myself has turned out to be mainly cleaning and kitchen work. *Da Stefano's* is a hub of activity, so there is plenty to do. Life is hard but, still, it's not the sort of poverty we had on the farm. There's plenty of food and if you work for it, you can get on well. I've heard stories of families who arrived with the clothes they wore on their backs and through grit and determination made lots of money running cafés in this part of Wales.

I fill the cigarette machine sometimes. And the jars of sweets, a bit of brightness in this grey country, with their jewelled mix of shapes and sizes. I've tried some, not like the sweets I had as a child, these ones are mostly made by factories in England. A few old men, regulars, sit in the corner with their cigarettes reading the newspaper and looking out at the passers-by. Some days, when I come through with supplies, I'm amazed how many people are packed in at the tables and I've found there's a pattern with the people who arrive at different times.

The mothers come in the morning, with their prams and toddlers, light up over a coffee and cake and have a good gossip. Some of them are young and pretty and Stefano enjoys joking with them and charming them with his flattery. They seem to like it and their own men are mostly not like that, after a day's work in the mines or factories or maybe studying in the evening at the Miners' Institute to better themselves. Stefano told me the cafe has been going for a long time, opened by his father when he came over before the Second World War and he's kept it traditional in his Papa's way. His father was interned during the war and his Mamma kept the café going then. Some of the café owners were on the ship that was torpedoed, The Andorra Star. I know about that. There is a memorial in Bardi with lots of names. Stefano talks about it all in a matter-of-fact voice. He says his Papa was welcomed back after the war by the people of the town. They love their Italian cafés here.

The layout reminds me of places at home, with the wooden tables and chairs, the pastries and coffee, the cosy fug of people not rushing anywhere. But it's strange at the same time, those red and brown sauces in plastic bottles and everyone speaking the language, so fast I can't understand. All in all, I don't feel part of it, not yet, but there's something comfortable and homely about it as well. Stefano says if I keep on improving my skills and learning English, he might let me go out the front in some months.

After school time the girls and boys from the grammar schools meet and giggle over a drink. It reminds me of home and my schooldays when Giuseppe and I would meet the girls under the castle walls. He always made them laugh with his jokes and loud voice while I watched in admiration, too shy to say much. Sweet memories.

Later in the day the miners come in after their shifts. They are parched and exhausted, but they give off a vitality, buzzing as though they've come from a war zone. I've seen the pit heads and I can't imagine what it would be like working underground in those dark and dank conditions. Signora Rossi tells me times are changing and many pits have closed. I know there are Italian men who have gone down to work alongside the Welsh but that would be my idea of hell after the mountain air and sunshine of home.

Sometimes there's a meeting of the Italian families to discuss politics or matters related to our community. I've begun to see that most of the people my age are second-generation Italians. They were born in Wales and have been to local schools; they speak perfect English as well as fluent Italian. But most of them have grandparents or relatives in the Bardi area and some visit in the summer holidays. It's strange. I knew all about this when I lived at home and heard neighbours mentioning relatives coming over; but it was other families, not us. Now I'm one of those people. A stranger in a strange land. I wonder when I might be able to go back. Not for a long time. I'll have to earn a lot more money on top of paying back the debts. Still, the homesickness, which made me feel ill when I first arrived, is beginning to leave me.

As the weeks go by, I'm finding I understand more English, enough to realise there is another language, called Welsh, which is completely different. It has combinations of letters which seem impossible to pronounce, but when I hear people speaking it, I like the song in their voices. And they are great singers. Stefano told me there are famous miners' male voice choirs and Tom Jones who lived close to Ponty in Treforest but is now so famous he lives in America. How strange that must be.

I send money back to Mamma and write letters telling her about all this. In the last one I sent, I realised I wasn't putting on a brave face just for her sake. What I was telling her and what I was feeling was getting closer. Father Bernardo's right. It takes time and patience.

Mamma writes every week and I reply. I phoned once, although it's too expensive to talk for long, and she has to go to La Pavone, the hotel in Bardi, at a set time to receive a call. Aunt Violetta does not have a telephone. In her letters Mamma tells me that she likes living with the family. She has a nice room in the house. She writes about Violetta's son and daughter, my cousins, who are married and live nearby, as though they are my brother and sister. That's strange but I suppose she has grown closer to them since I left. She also tells me Francesco's wife has ordered new furniture and Francesco has begun improvements on the farm, mending broken fences, fixing machinery and tools, tidying the fields ready to sow next Spring. In some ways I feel a little jealous. I don't have his training in agriculture. I couldn't turn things around like he has. Still, it's good news too, as Mamma will have a share of the profits, like we agreed at the start. Then there'll be more money to pay the debt.

From the café I look at the crowds walking past, their footsteps echoing on the pavement. Some of them are window shopping. Others are carrying bags from the Woolworths store in Taff Street or things for their children from the big toy shop called Garfield's. I've visited Woolworths and, if I had money to spare, there were things, like records or clothes, I would love to buy. Signora Rossi has a record player that the family bought for her and there's a shop called Rainbow Records. I pass it sometimes, but I never go in. That's not for me. Not yet. The farm seems a long way away. My life isn't about fields, animals and the seasons anymore. It's about industry and coal mining; busy streets; traffic; people with different ways of living and different languages.

As I'm cleaning the windows, a red mini roars up and screeches to a halt in front of the café. The driver jumps out and heads towards me. A 'Ciao' and he enters, closing the door so briskly the bell rings a few times.

Stefano's son. It must be. He's been away in London working with his uncle. He looks like Stefano, muscular and powerful. Wearing expensive-looking leather shoes, jeans and a red polo top. He doesn't look like he's going to work.

I go in and he's sitting at a table, smoking and chatting to one of the young mothers. He sees me. 'Hey, *ragazzo*. Bring me a coffee.' I glance at Stefano. He's beaming.

'This is Ricardo, my son. Get him whatever he wants, Angelo.'

I can see that the return of the prodigal son is going to change things. Ricardo and I glance at each other, then look away.

Olivia returns

The house shakes as the front door slams and a voice yells, 'Mamma. Where are you? I'm home.'

I'm upstairs, sorting my things while I have a chance. I'm happy Olivia's back, even though it means the discomfort of the sofa. I hope she remembers her promise to help me improve my English. Stefano says, until I can talk to the customers with more confidence, I'm to stay in the kitchen and wash up, prepare the food and collect deliveries. General dogsbody. I go to the top of the stairs and Olivia's there at the bottom, looking up at me. She's got a bag in each hand and another slung over her shoulder. She seems to fill the narrow hallway and almost knocks the mirror off the wall when she moves.

Olivia reminds me of the girls at home. She's got dark hair and beautiful eyes, huge, and, at this moment, twinkling as she notices how shy I am. She seems to bubble with life and she's always smiling, even on the darkest, most miserable day, like today.

'Angelo. Where's Mamma? I thought she'd be here.'

'I think she's in the café with Signora Davies. She's been trying to persuade your Mamma to join her at the clothes factory.'

Olivia shook her head. 'Mama is fine for money now you are her lodger and why aren't you there anyway? I thought Stefano had you tied to that kitchen sink. He's not actually let you have time off, has he?'

'I was sick this morning. He's afraid in case I pass something on to the customers.'

'So, you've got a day free. Wonderful. What are you going to do with the rest of the afternoon?'

I frown. What can I do? I'm supposed to be sick, although, in fact, the sickness passed by midday. I should have gone to the café then, but I still feel lethargic and light-headed.

'Let's go out.' Olivia drops her bags on the floor and grabs my arm, leading me towards the door.

'No.'

She can tell I'm determined about that as I pull away, so, instead, we go into the front room. The fire's unlit but there's that lingering smell of coal dust. The window looks out on to the street and the hills in the distance. A sofa, stool and a side table are all the furniture the room can hold. There's also a mantlepiece over the fireplace with family photographs. The window is shrouded in net curtains, blocking what little light there is.

'So, why can't you go out? You're not sick now, are you?'

'No, I feel much better but if I'm seen out on the streets Stefano will go crazy with me. I must stay in today. Besides, I need to clear my things out of your room.'

'Oh, don't worry about that. You can do it later. If you can't go out, then I'll just have to stay and look after you. Poorly boy.' She pouts then and winks. 'Come and sit down on the sofa with me.'

She pats the seat. Too close. I can smell her perfume. Something fresh and sweet like summer flowers. She bends towards me a little and her hair brushes my face. I try to move away but she presses her leg against mine and laughs when I blush. What am I supposed to do? The room feels almost claustrophobic. I look around and a photograph of Signora Rossi and her husband on their wedding day stares back at me. Accusing. From this photograph Olivia looks more like her father than her mother. In this awkward situation I can't think straight and she's teasing me now.

'Oh dear, you're so shy. I'll have to give you some tips on how to deal with the girls. I'm sure you've already had a few after you, so handsome, with those gorgeous brown eyes. Have you got a girlfriend, little Angelo?'

I can feel the hot, betraying flush all over my face and neck and try to swallow. My voice seems to have got lost somewhere between chest and throat and I shake my head. At last I manage to stammer, 'No. I've no time for that and no money. I send money home so there's little left. And the language. I don't know what to say.'

Olivia moves away a little. One of the springs in the sofa makes a pinging sound and she laughs.

'I am naughty. I shouldn't flirt with you. I just get so bored the moment I come home. There's always something to do in Cardiff. You'll have to come down sometime and I'll show you the sights. There's a castle.'

'Like Bardi?'

'Not so ancient, I think. It's not on top of a hill either – but it's interesting to learn about Cardiff and its history. There are parks, museums and shops. Lots of shops. Many more than here in Ponty. I love it.'

It all sounds so different and I long to escape for a little while to explore this new country I'm living in. I've been for walks up on the hills surrounding Pontypridd, looking away to the distance toward mountains called the Brecon Beacons, but I've seen no other town. My world is made up of the inside of the café and the narrow streets on my way to and from work.

'It... it sounds very interesting.'

'One day we'll go together but... I know – how about we start your English lessons.'

Olivia moves from the sofa and goes to her bag, scrabbling about to find a pad of paper and a pencil. Although it's still early afternoon, it's already dark in the room and she switches on the light. A yellow glow illuminates everything but the air still feels damp and cold. She kneels and lights the fire in the grate and the flames soon lick around the coals. There's not much warmth from it yet, but in a little while the room will be more comfortable. I see with relief that Olivia has switched off the flirting.

'Right. Let's start with the basics. You know how to greet people and a bit of the vocabulary around food from working in the café. What about parts of the body? She points to her wrist. What do you call this, *polso*, in English?'

'Um.'

She writes the word.

'I don't know how you would say that. English spelling is so hard.'

'Wrist. Say it like this – r-i-s-t.' She exaggerates the sounds, elongating them, exaggerating and then blending them together. I copy her. After a few attempts I get it.

'Wrist.'

She nods in approval. I'm conscious of my accent which is so different from hers. She's been brought up here, part of the community. She sounds more Welsh than Italian, even though her family speak Italian at home. The lesson continues with a lot of mistakes and laughter. We're having so much fun, we don't hear the door open. We both jump at the sound of a rough male voice.

'What's going on here?' Ricardo, Stefano's son. He doesn't like me, I know. Catching me here laughing when I should be in work is terrible. He'll tell his father and then there'll be big trouble. I sit caught red-handed, a feeling of dread paralysing me and unable to speak. Olivia tosses her hair and, in that teasing voice of hers, responds, taking immediate control of the situation.

'Oh, I came home to find poor Angelo with his head down the toilet. I've been trying to distract him by teaching him some English. He's pretty hopeless, though.'

It's the perfect answer. I don't mind that Olivia has made fun of me. Like Olivia, Ricardo has been to school here, so his English is perfect, spoken with that special lilt the Welsh seem to have. She knows the way to deal with Ricardo is to make him feel superior.

'I wondered if you were home yet. Papa asked me to call in to check on the pup,' he sneers at me, 'and I could hear the laughter outside. Fancy the cinema later? We could sit in the back seats. Share some popcorn?' He's winking at Olivia now and I feel it's time to get out of the way.

'I… I think I'll go and lie down for a while. I'm sure you two have things to talk about.'

I get to my feet. Despite the fact Ricardo is a year older than me, I'm more than an inch taller. He pulls himself up and squares his shoulders.

'You watch yourself. If I catch you making moves on my girl…' The threat is obvious. He raises a fist and I back away. The last thing I want, or need, is a fight with the boss's son.

'For goodness sake, Ric. Stop acting like a gangster boy. You're not in the mafia. You watch too many movies.'

'Oh yeah?' He puts an arm around Olivia's waist and, while he's distracted by her, I make my escape. I hear him muttering to her.

'Mmmm. You smell nice. What time's your Mamma expected home? Time for a little…'

I glance into the room as I make my way upstairs and see him nuzzle into Olivia's neck. She's watching me over his shoulder, and I imagine her eyes tell me she's allowing him to get close so I can make my escape. From upstairs I hear the mumble of their voices and then the front door opens again.

'Olivia. *La mia bambina. Finalmente a casa.*' Signora Rossi's voice reaches me in its excitement. Then a pause before, 'Ricardo. I didn't expect to see you here.'

'I called to check that Angelo's feeling okay. I'm glad to see your daughter back as well. I'm taking her out to the pictures later.'

I can imagine the smug look on his face and the smile on Signora Rossi's face. She thinks Ricardo would be a good match for her daughter. Somehow, I don't think Olivia is quite as sure.

I'll have to remember not to be too friendly with Olivia when I see her out and about and especially in the café. Ricardo is a possessive and jealous man and I don't need trouble.

Ricardo plays dirty

After three months here my English is coming on well and I'm getting to know one or two of the regular customers. Even Stefano is satisfied with how hard I work and how eager I am to learn; and I've managed to put aside a little money to buy Mamma a present for Christmas. It'll be difficult to be apart for the first time, but I have found her a speciality from Wales, a little wooden carving, called a love spoon. I hope she likes it. I found it in the market. It's even more busy than usual with stalls selling Christmas items, toys, sweets and clothes.

We've had frosts over the last weeks. I like the cold weather. It seems to scour and clean the landscape. Some clear blue skies, too, and now I have a day off each month, I've been exploring. I like the path by the River Taff, very peaceful. The water at the edge is frozen today. Further on I find huge standing stones and gaze in wonder. A lady walking her dog stops to talk. People here like to chat and she tells me these stones are very ancient.

'They're called rock stones, lovely. Been here forever, they have. And see that old bridge down there?' She points. 'At one time it had the longest single span in the world. What you think of that then? Didn't know Ponty was such a grand place, did you now?' She laughs and carries on her way, pulling the elderly terrier behind her.

My favourite walk is one which Olivia told me about, where you go high up above the town, seeing sheep and bracken and the white rock, Graigwen, near where she told me there was once a pilgrim's way. It gives me the sort of feeling I had at home climbing the hills, although parts of the landscape here are scarred from the history of coalmining. At the highest point it's like a bird's eye view, and Olivia told me on a clear day you can see as far as the coast, the Bristol Channel.

Things are tricky at work though. We're busier than ever and there's enough to do for me, Stefano and Ricardo. But, although I keep out of his way as much as I can, it's hard when you work with someone; and

Ricardo really has it in for me. I know he doesn't like me because I show him up. Work hard, always on time, stay late. But, after all, he's the owner's son with nothing to prove. And then there's the business with Olivia.

'You watch out, boy. Olivia's my girl. You put a foot wrong and I'll kill you.'

He's seen us laughing together as we walk to mass. One time he pushed me against a cupboard and pressed his arm against my neck so that I could hardly breathe. I can still feel the bruise. '*Mamma mia!*' Signora Rossi says when she sees my black eye. Olivia looks concerned and I tell them it's nothing, that I tripped over something, but I don't think they believe me. Stefano must have some idea what's going on but ignores it.

Olivia and I carry on with the English lessons in the house, being careful to arrange them when Signora Rossi is there. We laugh so much; and Signora Rossi says she is learning things about the English language she didn't know before. Olivia makes learning English fun and I'm sure that's why I'm improving so quickly. A few times Ricardo drops by to see Olivia but, with Signora Rossi there, he's polite. Still, he sees how Signora Rossi approves of me, which adds fuel to the fire of his dislike. His face betrays his jealousy. His scowl's dark as the slag heaps.

I've known my fair share of bullying with Papa, but there's something nasty about Ricardo, a mean streak. If he doesn't get his own way, he has a terrible temper. Stefano is harsh, very harsh, but he's not cruel. I wouldn't like to be employed by Ricardo. Bad enough working alongside him. He makes threats under his breath all the time, when Stefano isn't around. Olivia says the gangster language he uses is from watching the movies, but I don't want to risk it. I need this job. There's the Barbieri family back home to think of, too, and if I don't send them money, well, who knows . . .

Ricardo asks Olivia out again a few times, but I notice she's always found a reason not to accept. I can tell he's getting frustrated and, of course, he's taking it out on me. Trying to get me into trouble. He drops a pile of dishes while we're doing the washing up, breaks a few and shouts out, so his father can hear in the front of the shop, 'Idiot, you'll have to pay for those broken dishes.' Stefano hurries in and looks from one to the other of us. I'm relieved he doesn't seem to believe it's all my fault, but he has had enough and the threat in his voice is clear as he heads back to the customers, 'You two better sort this out – or there'll be trouble.'

School breaks up for the Christmas holidays today and I'm serving Gwen Thomas and her friend, Dilys Jones. They like to sit at the back, out of the way, so they can rock the prams or take the babies out to bounce. They tell me they won't be in for a while now, but they'll see me around. I've just put down their coffees when I sense Ricardo coming in. I'm always on my guard with him, just to be on the safe side, one step ahead if I can.

The next thing I know he's on me, pushing me back towards one of the prams. I stumble and put my arm out to the wall, so I don't fall into it, but my foot catches the wheel. The baby starts crying from the shock and Mrs Thomas leaps up.

'Hey, boys, what's going on?' Stefano rushes across from where he's been chatting to a couple of our regulars, elderly guys who come in every day for a catch up on the newspaper and a bit of man's talk with the boss.

Ricardo looks at me, furious.

‘It’s him,’ jabbing his finger in my direction, ‘Ever since he’s arrived, things have gone wrong.’

Stefano doesn’t waste words. He puts a hand to each of our backs and propels us out of the front and into the kitchen.

‘It’s girl trouble, isn’t it?’ Stefano glowers at us both but then his finger points to Ricardo. ‘Sniffing around that Rossi girl again ever since you got back from London.’

‘She’s been brushing me off. Only started after he arrived.’ Ricardo gives me a look of hate. He’s getting worked up again, smells of alcohol too. I eye the distance between him and the back door. He puts his hand in his pocket and my muscles tense, ready, but he brings a box out of his pocket.

‘I gave her this watch, cost a lot, but she said she couldn’t take it. Said she wanted to be “a friend”, didn’t want to go out with me. She’s a two-timing slut.’

‘I don’t want to hear any more of this nonsense.’ Stefano shouts. ‘Go home and sober up. Angelo, get back to work.’

When I get to my digs at the end of my shift, Signora Rossi is putting sheets into the twin-tub washing machine. It's a luxury Mamma cannot afford. She used to take her washing out to the trough at the back of the house and pump the water. How much harder life was for her on the farm. I can tell by the way Signora Rossi is huffing and puffing she's heard about the fight.

'I change my mind about Stefano's boy. Coming here smelling of booze. He's not good for my Olivia. She going to stay with her sister for a few days. I speak to Stefano. That boy need to behave. Then he can see my girl again.'

I'm back in the comfort of a proper bed, but I don't lie in it easily. My first Christmas away and trouble still follows me.

But I don't have much time to think about how this Christmas is going to be very different from last year. We're busy in the café up until late on Christmas Eve. Ricardo never likes to close his doors and a steady stream of people come in to the end; the last Christmas shoppers wanting a cup of tea or coffee and cake, travelling in to buy presents and get posh Christmas food from the Co-op in Ponty. When we close up that evening, I make a phone call to mamma. She's crying. The first Christmas without me. I try to reassure her, even though I feel the tiredness in my voice must be obvious. She's sent me a big parcel with the Bertorellis who've travelled over to visit cousins here.

We attend Mass and I say my prayers, remembering mamma and pappa, and trying to be grateful for the good things in my new life. And later I do enjoy the festival day spent with Signora Rossi, Olivia, Sophia and Glyn, her son-in-law. We have lots to eat, sit around the fire, watch television, chat and tell jokes. My first real holiday since arriving in this country. But, before I know it, my alarm's going off and I'm peeling myself out of bed and off to work again.

The days go into weeks, then months, and soon it is my first Spring in Wales. I am learning about the business, how to speak to people who come into the café, more about the customs of this place. My English is becoming more fluent and I can even speak some words of greeting in Welsh. Father Bernardo would be proud of what I have achieved over the last months. But on Friday and Saturday nights, listening to the shouts, catcalls and laughter from the Polytechnic students at turning out time from the pub, I wonder, Is this it? Is this all my life will be?

Two Years Later

The dance

Signora Rossi is in a fluster. Olivia is coming home for the dance in Merthyr and a friend is coming with her to stay for the weekend.

'Oh, *Mamma mia.* She bring home a girl. English girl. What I do, Angelo? This girl, what do I know about her? Nothing. I ask my Olivia, "Where does she sleep? What does she like to eat? What do her parents do? Will she be alright here, in this little house?" But Olivia, she just laugh at her poor Mamma.'

Despite many years living in the valley, Signora Rossi, has a strong accent and, when flustered, mixes up her words.

I try to calm her. 'I'm sure, if she's a friend of Olivia's, she'll be very nice. Don't worry. It'll only be for a couple of days. She can have Olivia's room and Olivia can sleep on the sofa. I'll ask Stefano if I can put a sleeping bag in the storeroom at the café.'

'*Mamma mia.* No, no, no. I can't have that. What would they say? The neighbours will think I am bad landlady, putting my best boy out on the street. It will not do. Olivia can come in with me.'

I think about Signora Rossi and how loudly she snores. I'm not sure what Olivia will think but it's not my place to argue.

'I'm usually so tired I could sleep on the branch of a tree.'

Signora Rossi laughs at that. 'You're no bird, Angelo. You fall off.' She starts to laugh and rocks on her feet at the idea. Lifting a corner of her apron to her eyes she says, 'You're a good boy. I speak to Stefano about you. He still not treat you right sometimes, I think.'

Later

I feel a surge of excitement. The Italian community is buzzing. I'm on my way to the dance at Merthyr. Olivia will be there, bringing her friend. They were delayed leaving Cardiff, so Ricardo is giving them a lift. He's still hoping Olivia will relent and go out with him on a more permanent basis. She goes for a drink with him sometimes but it's obvious to everyone except Ricardo that he doesn't have a hope. I don't think Olivia wants to settle down. I don't blame her; and Ricardo might be the boss's son, a catch, and seem charming to women, but that's only if he gets his own way.

My clothes are clean and pressed and Signora Rossi is sitting in the front seat in Stefano's car. She's bullied him into giving us both a lift, but I can see by the way his hands grip the steering wheel he's not pleased that I'm there.

The journey isn't too long, and I can see green fields as well as the grey slag heaps that dot this land. A landscape so different from home. Will I ever go back? What will things be like there when I do? Signora Rossi turns round to me from her place in the front, interrupting my daydreaming as I watch the countryside go past.

'Many pretty girls at the dance. Maybe you click. Yes?' I blush, much to my dismay. I can't seem to stop the tide of pink that seeps up my chest and face. I know that many of the Italian Mammas think of me as good husband material. But, like Olivia, I'm not ready to settle yet. Plus, I haven't met the right girl.

Signora Rossi is bubbling and chattering away. I try to pretend I'm listening.

'Is such a good night. You have fun, you see. Like Italy. Much dancing, much laughing.'

Stefano decides to join in. 'You've just gotta watch out for the smart boys, the ones who've been away. They reckon they're better than us café folk. Just because they got a bit of money, they like to lord it over us. Last time Ricardo lost it and ended up in a nasty fight. Got a black eye.'

I think how much I'd like to give Ricardo a black eye and feel envy for the person who managed to deal the blow. I pretend astonishment, while suppressing a smile.

'What happened?'

'Some fancy lad from the south, London way, demanded Ricardo got him a drink. So, he went to the bar, got a pint and poured it over the boy's head. Unfortunately, he got a punch in before Ricardo saw what was coming. He had quite a bruiser. Fights don't happen too often but watch out for yourself.'

'That's awful.' I make a mental note not to tangle with anyone, especially if goaded. Smile and walk away, Papa used to say.

'Who's playing tonight? I heard they'd brought over a band from Italy.'

'Yes. I think it's Andrea Bellagio. Traditional music and then the disco. I hope you've been practising your moves, my friend.' Stefano wiggles a little in the driving seat and starts singing a popular song from the radio – Seasons in the Sun. Signora Rossi giggles like a schoolgirl. I wonder if they're flirting. They're both widowed. What would she see in a man like that? What do women want? I often feel I don't understand them at all.

In the entrance to the hall the nerves kick in and my stomach lurches. My palms get all sweaty, so I flatten the front of my shirt and then put my hands into my pockets, trying to look relaxed, casual. If only. At least, I know I look groomed with Signora Rossi's ironing of my clothes and I bought some aftershave, so I smell good. It's called English Leather, but it smells nothing like leather. The adverts say it's what women like. I hope so.

The place is vast. The lights are slightly dimmed and a huge glitterball in the centre gives the impression of stardust falling. Lots of tables are set out, each with a vivid purple tablecloth, the colour brash against the browns and oranges of the carpeted area. Chairs are placed randomly as if the person organising things had been distracted. It looks like everyone from the Italian community is here, from the elderly, like Signora Sartori, eighty last birthday, to babes in arms. I feel my heart warming and I begin to calm down. Although this country is still alien to me, these people are not. The music starts and I feel my spirits lift and my feet tap in time. Stefano is at a table piled high with sandwiches. He calls me over.

'Angelo. Come, come. A drink.'

He's a different person here. No longer grumpy and unfriendly, like he often is when not with customers. No longer the café owner, chatty and charming either. It's as if he's shed his responsibilities for a while. He presses a glass of beer into my hand and then, with a wave, summons Signora Rossi to get up and dance.

As they move around the floor in the swirl of people, I see Olivia has arrived. Ricardo is hovering over her, as usual. The atmosphere feels electric, but unpredictable, when they're together. She could easily find someone better. But what do I know? I don't even have a girlfriend.

Beside them is a girl I've never seen before. It must be the friend from college who's staying with us. Her blonde hair gleams like gold, lit up by one of spotlights, and she has a beautiful smile. She *is* beautiful.

Olivia's seen me and makes her way through the crowd with her friend in tow. Ricardo watches with a deep frown on his face. If looks could kill I would already be dead.

'Angelo. Mamma said you'd be here. She's hoping you'll find a nice Italian girl to hitch up with.'

'Well, she's given up on you then. No nice Italian boys at that college of yours or are you sticking with home-grown?' I glance towards Ricardo. 'He's watching us.'

With a toss of her long dark hair Olivia throws her head back and laughs. 'Poor Mamma. The last thing I want is to get married and end up cooking pasta forever. I want to live – be a film star or a singer. Teaching is only a stopgap. It keeps Mamma happy thinking I'll have a steady job until I find a man.'

She swings around in a circle, laughing and waving her arms, taking up more space than she should. Her friend says nothing but smiles. Now that they are close beside me, I can see her blue eyes sparkling, maybe with amusement, as she takes in the scene around her. As if remembering where she is, and seeing my eyes on her friend, Olivia shrugs and nods towards the other girl.

'This is my friend, Catherine Chadwick. She *really* wants to be a teacher, would you believe?' She turns to Catherine. 'Angelo's my mother's lodger. That's why there are those y-fronts, shirts and socks in there.'

Catherine's eyes widen. 'Oh no. I didn't know it was your room. I'm so sorry. Where are you sleeping?'

I open my mouth to answer but Olivia interrupts. 'On the sofa, of course. I'm in Mamma's room with her. God, I hope she doesn't snore too much tonight.'

I feel the colour rise in my face, yet again. This blushing is an affliction I could do without. Catherine looks horrified. 'But, that's awful. I'm sure I could find a hotel or… '

'Don't be silly. We're in the valleys – not London. How many hotels do you think there are around here?' Olivia is enjoying herself. 'I promised you it would be an experience. Quite a far cry from your parents' mansion in Kent.'

'It's not a mansion. It's just a four-bedroom detached …'

'Yeah. In one of the most expensive areas of the south east with several acres. Daddy's in finance and has a little cottage in France just for weekends. Don't try to pretend, Catherine. This is slumming for you.' Olivia's tone isn't joking anymore.

Catherine looks a little taken aback and bites her lip.

‘One day I’ll have a house like that.’ The words come unbidden from my mouth. My dreams laid bare in front of a stranger. What am I doing?

Olivia snorts and joins Ricardo to get a drink. Catherine lingers, giving me a serious look.

‘Ambition is a good quality to have… but you’ll have to work hard, you know.’

‘I’m not afraid of hard work. I have ideas, plans. I don’t want to live my life working in a café. Cleaning, cooking, waiting on tables. I want more than that.’ I pause, waiting for a response. Will she laugh at me? Why does it seem important that she doesn’t? This girl is different. I’m curious about her. I take a breath and ask, ‘Why do you let Olivia say things like that about your family? It’s rude.’

She shrugs her shoulders. ‘I think she feels a little embarrassed at the difference in our backgrounds. It’s a defensive thing, I suppose. But she needn’t worry. I love it here. Everyone is so friendly. Money isn’t everything.’

She moves off to where Olivia is talking to a group of girls. I watch as Olivia pulls her friend into the circle and links arms. I find myself watching Catherine most of the night. I think she’s aware as sometimes she turns and smiles. The folk dances finish. There's a DJ, playing records. I laugh as some of the elderly matrons dance to the Loco-Motion. They're having so much fun it's infectious. Then Olivia pulls me on to the floor for the Conga and tells me to hold onto Catherine to make up the line. As I grasp Catherine's tiny waist, and breathe in her fresh perfume, while weaving in and out and around the hall, I know this girl is special. This is someone I want to get to know better.

Bardi

My Mamma matchmakes

The rickety bus from Parma trundles into the square and it's as though I'd never been away. I wanted to hitch a lift, but I knew Mamma would worry about safety and she has enough to worry about. Nearly two years but everything looks the same, baked in the sun. I'd forgotten how hot it is and even just sitting here, not moving, I'm sweating. I'm exhausted too, but excitement and anticipation has kept me going. The square looks the same with the concrete benches and the dusty, acrid smell from the plane trees. There are the familiar pots of bright flowers; and still the old ladies standing together on the shaded side of the street, watching with suspicious eyes and complaining about the *stranieri,* strangers. I wonder if I am a stranger now.

I walk as fast as I can towards the villa where Aunt Violetta lives. I hurry as my steps take me along Via dell Emigrante, Via dei Carpini and out of the centre. It's mid-afternoon. The shutters are closed in the town, the sun high in the sky, and I smell the familiar scents of late July, cows, dust, flowers in blossom, citrus. I'm sweating so much that when I get near Aunt Violetta's house, carrying my bag with clothes for ten days and the presents, I pause to get my breath back and wipe my face, standing in the shade of the tree opposite. Everything is quiet, not even a dog barking. Surely, they're expecting me?

I'd forgotten how big her house is, three storeys, how solid with its old stones, wooden shutters and the curved, ancient door. In Ponty you'd have to be rich to have a house that size.

'Angelo!' Aunt Violetta hurries towards me. Her basket squashes awkwardly into my side as we embrace. 'We thought you were arriving in the evening. *Entra. Entra.*'

It's wonderfully cool once we get inside and Aunt Violetta takes me through to the back of the house. I look up at the high rafters and the painted patterns on the walls. This house is more lavish than the farm, but it all feels so familiar.

'Your Mamma's having a rest. She'll be down as soon as she hears your voice.' Aunt Violetta puts a glass of lemonade and a generous slice of *Torta Barozzi* on the table next to me and pulls up a chair opposite. For a moment there's quiet, apart from the ticking of the clock. Then we hear heavy footsteps on the floor above.

'There. I told you she'd be down. Let me look at you properly now.' Aunt Violetta smiles. She's the lively one, the fortunate one, happily married to a wealthy man. That's what Mamma always told me, anyway.

'The life there in Wales suits you. You've grown taller and filled out – although you are pale. Not too much sun there, eh?'

'Angelo, Angelo.' Mamma stands in the doorway looking at me as though she can't believe her eyes. Two years since we've seen each other but she still can't hug me like Aunt Violetta did. '*Ragazzo mio, figlio mio*. How you have changed.'

I laugh, feel awkward. She seems to be almost accusing me of this. What did she expect? It's been a long time, tough, and I've learnt so much.

'Mamma. You look well.' I go over and kiss her on both cheeks. She's put on weight and looks more relaxed. 'I've brought you this, all the way from Wales.'

I feel bad because, when she opens the soft Welsh wool shawl, she cries.

Later, after supper, I go for a walk in the cool of the evening. Although I'm exhausted, I need to stretch my legs before I can hope to sleep up in the attic of Aunt Violetta's house. It's a room twice the size of my old room on the farm. And that's where my legs take me, almost without having to think. Our farm. There are lights blazing all over the house, the vegetable patch looks well-tended and there are several goats grazing in the fields. I find myself looking at the place like a stranger. When we were home, we only had a light on where we needed it, meagre livestock and the vegetable patch never seemed to thrive. Perhaps Papa's drinking and my lack of interest in farming were at the heart of it. I don't go any closer in case I meet Francesco, turn back in some haste, and head towards the town.

Before my head hits the pillow and I fall into a deep sleep, I make a promise to myself that I will never go back. At least not in the same way. Francesco knows a better method and could teach me. But there are still too many bad memories of struggling along with Papa. It's a comfort to see how well my cousin is looking after everything and the place is looking more like a proper home than it ever did when I lived there with Mamma and Papa.

The next morning, Mamma says we are to visit her friend Luisa. We've been invited for coffee and cake. As we walk together in the early morning sun, Mamma leaning on my arm, I vaguely remember Luisa, seeing her sometimes in church. To be honest, I'm glad of something to do. I feel restless and out of place. I'm used to getting up early and working hard through the day at the café, so all this free time seems strange. And meeting cousins and family is tiring, trying to tell them about my life. It's a pleasure to be at home and to speak my mother tongue all the time, but there are so many things I can't really find words to explain, like the mining and industry, the food, the whole way of living. Thinking about it here it seems alien, but in Wales it is familiar to me now.

'Carlotta will be at Luisa's house too.' Mamma squeezes my arm. 'You remember her, a clever girl, very pretty. She went away to study and is back working in an office job. She speaks good English, you know. You can talk together.'

I haven't been away from Bardi so long that I can't recognise the signs of matchmaking and my heart sinks.

Catherine. An image of her at the dance comes to me; her wonderful blue eyes and mischievous smile, her confident, independent way of dealing with things. What would Mamma make of her? Everything about Catherine Chadwick shows her so clearly to be from a different class, and wealthy. Mamma would be intimidated. And what about Catherine? What would she think? I glance at Mamma and see her wispy grey hair, hands knotted with arthritis, her back bent from hard work. But she's a clever woman herself. She could have done a lot more if she'd had the chance.

We arrive at Luisa's house and it's time to be polite over coffee and cake.

The ten days of my visit pass all too quickly, almost as in a dream, but I'm glad, one afternoon, to have the chance of meeting up with Giuseppe. I tell him I am paying off the debts as much as I can, but I still felt alarmed when I saw Signor Barbieri in the distance one time. I went down another street to avoid him. 'Low life,' Giuseppe said dismissively, although I think to myself it's easier for him to be so firm when he doesn't owe the man any money. But the main reason I want to talk to Giuseppe is about the matchmaking problem. He laughs at first and says I'm making something big out of nothing.

'No, I'm sure, Giuseppe. I'm not imagining it. Mamma wants me to get engaged to Carlotta – you remember her – marry, have kids, maybe stay in Wales for a while and then come back to the farm. But that's not going to happen. I have my own plans. I still dream of travel, of starting a business, making money.'

We've gone for a hike along the Via Abati, testing ourselves over the nine-kilometre walk. Steep climbs, beautiful views and horses grazing in some of the pastures. Giuseppe is home for the summer from university; and it's such a relief to speak to someone outside the family. We sit on a rock looking out at the blue haze of the mountains in the distance, the buzz of insects and the smell of grass and herbs in the air around us.

'Is it just the farming, *mio amico*, or is there a pretty girl back in Wales?'

Giuseppe is a proper student now, with his round glasses, beard and long hair, but his teasing smile is just the same as when we were kids in school together. And he knows me. 'Carlotta's a sweet girl, pretty and all that, but, you're right, there is someone…'

'I knew it. Tell me then…'

'She's English, doesn't live in Pontypridd. Her parents are rich.'

'So, what does that matter – if you love each other?'

'I don't know, Giuseppe. I don't know how she feels about me. I've hardly met her more than a few times and I'm still learning English.'

'I've faith in you, Angelo. If you want something enough, you'll make it happen.' He slaps me on the back like he always does when he's encouraging me.

'Perhaps ... I hope so. Only three more days before I leave. Mamma seems to be obsessed with the idea of me getting married. What shall I tell her?'

'Only you know that, *mio amico*.' He jumps up. 'You'll find a way. *L'amore domina senza regole*. All's fair in love and war. For now, I'm starving. Let's see how quickly we can get back.'

The question of Mamma and my future is postponed, but later that week, as I start my long journey back to Pontypridd, my brain is whirling, trying to work it all out. I feel unsettled and unsure of my place in the world.

Pontypridd

My return to Wales

Before, when I was dreaming on the farm of my future, before my life changed and Papa died, I thought travelling would be fun, but in truth, it's very tiring and even boring at times. I watch the countryside pass by, the clouds floating in the sky, free and unencumbered by worry, and my body aches for sleep. Deep sleep in a proper bed. I've dozed on buses and boats but I long to lie down, stretch and sleep for eight hours or more. My eyes feel as though they are full of sand. This bus smells of exhaust fumes and body odour. I know I must smell too, in the same clothes, unshaven, only a brief splash of water on my face when I was on the ferry. As soon as I get to Pontypridd, I'm going to wash and then have some sleep. Tomorrow I'll be back in the café. There'll be no rest then.

The rain has started again and, as we approach the town, all I see is bleakness. It's like changing from colour film to black and white. The heat and colours of

Italy; clear blue skies; orange and yellow rooftops; the sounds of the cicadas; the scent of rosemary and thyme and the still warmth of the night is replaced by grey, damp and cold. I'm homesick for Italy already. I hope it won't be as bad this time as when I first arrived in Ponty.

I trudge from the bus station along Morgan Street through the town and then the uphill climb to Vaughan Street. The house with its front door opening onto the street seems smaller than ever. But at last I have arrived back after all my travelling. I open the door and go in, dumping my bag in the hall with a long sigh. Here, in this place, few people lock their doors, it seems. Everybody knows everybody else and few people have anything worth stealing anyway. The way of life for them is to pop into each other's houses for a chat and a cup of tea. In my exhausted state, it all feels so strange again.

The radio's blaring out a pop tune. It sounds like Gordon Lightfoot. I surprise myself with my knowledge. I suppose listening in the café has had an influence. I can't imagine that it's Signora Rossi listening to that sort of music. Of course – Olivia. It has to be. I smile when I see her friendly face.

‘Angelo. Welcome home.’ She runs up to kiss me on both cheeks and then draws back, her eyes twinkling as usual, as she says, ‘You look shattered – and you smell.’ She wrinkles her nose but smiles as she says it, so I know there’s no offence to be taken. She’s just telling the truth. I’m aware of it myself. I nod, too weary to make comment.

‘Go through and have a wash and change your clothes. Mamma’s out shopping, but I’ll heat you some soup and bread. Then you need to go and lie down.’

It’s pleasant being fussed over. Olivia and I have grown to like one another as good friends and since Ricardo’s gone back to London to work with his uncle things are easier all round. Stefano has, grudgingly, begun to give me more responsibility too. He can’t do everything, and he’s developed ulcers on his leg which make him even more bad-tempered, but also in need of help. I was surprised when he allowed me to go home to Italy, but I think Signora Rossi may have put some pressure on him. And its wasn’t such a busy time. No students and people away on holiday.

I feel a sudden warmth at the thought of Signora Rossi’s kindness. In this house, at least, there is solace and welcome. I eat the soup with too much haste, but my eyelids are so heavy I fear I may not be able to stay awake long enough to finish it. Olivia sends me upstairs to lie down on her bed. I know it will be the sofa for me while she's home, but it's the middle of the afternoon so I can rest for a few hours. I sink into the sweet-smelling pillows and sleep. A deep, dreamless sleep.

When I waken the sun is streaming through a gap in the curtains and I can hear Signora Rossi singing in the kitchen and the rattle of pots and pans. At first, I don't know where I am. Confused and bleary, I see I'm still in my clothes, crumpled now. My belly rumbles. It must be dinner time. I go downstairs. In the front room, Olivia is sitting on the sofa with a blanket wrapped around her, looking sleepy. Signora Rossi hears my feet on the stairs and comes to meet me, throwing her arms around me and pressing me to her ample bosom. There's a delicious smell of fresh-brewed coffee in the air.

'Angelo. I was going to wake you. I thought you dead, so long sleep. Breakfast ready.'

'Breakfast? But…'

'You were out cold. It seemed a shame to disturb you. You looked so sweet.' Olivia is teasing me now.

I glance at the clock on the mantlepiece. 'I must have slept for over twelve hours.'

'Fifteen more like. That bed of mine must be comfortable.'

I feel the familiar colour start to rise and Olivia notices and laughs. 'Don't worry. You're back on the sofa tonight.'

In the café nothing has changed. There are some fresh summer days, not fierce heat like it was when I work out on the fields in the old days. Still, I wonder why I'm here, working in a cafe. A stranger. But, back home I feel a stranger too now, everyone looking at me in the street and talking about me behind their hands. I can imagine the whispers. 'It's Enrico's son. You remember all that fuss after he died, the debts. He's living in Wales now.' I've only been away for two years but already things have changed. Life moves on.

People I know from school are married, they've jobs, babies. Giuseppe tells me he's going to move to Genoa for further studies. Even Uncle Carlo seems different. 'Well, Angelo. You've filled out. Grown up. No longer a boy. Ready for a wife, eh?' Mamma's been talking to him, I'm sure. I've escaped the match-making – for now. No doubt next year there'll be more pressure: settle, take on the farm again, marry a local girl. And I know, even if I stay in Wales, they expect me to marry a girl from home. I sigh at the thought of it all as I get ready for a long, hard day at work.

Stefano is as grumpy as usual. No warm greeting from him as I enter. Just a gruff, 'Get the vegetables prepared, boy.' At least there's no Ricardo. As I set about peeling, I have wondered if, with Ricardo out of the way, it'll mean more opportunities for me. Stefano's getting older he'll need someone to take over management. He's not good with the accounts. I'm excellent with figures. Perhaps I can help with that? But. . .who am I kidding? He'll suck the life out of me and then hand everything over to his son, or one of his cousins up the valley. Then again, Ricardo's well settled with his uncle in London now, so he won't want to take over this café in the back of beyond. My head spins with ideas, plans, dreams. There may be a chance…

'Customers.' Stefano's voice breaks through my reverie. I go into the front of the café and see the handful of women who usually come in on Monday mornings.

Stefano is beaming at them, winking and making cooing noises at the babies. He's like the character in that story Olivia told me about, Jekyll and Hyde. They all call him Steve and think he's wonderful. At the dance in the Spring he treated me well. But I know better. I see the other side. The tough businessman who has no time for sentiment when it comes to work.

I serve the customers and then don my apron again. I swear if I had 100 lire for every potato I've peeled since coming to this town I'd have paid off all the debts. I think about that for a moment, my hands red from the water and my heart cold with rage. But what else can I do? What choice do I have?

'You'll have to make up for lost time, boy.'

'What do you mean?'

'You've been away for a couple of weeks. How do you think I've managed all this time?' He waits, watching me with his beady eyes. I shrug my shoulders. I haven't given it a thought. 'I had to get someone in, pay them too. You owe me. No time off until you've made up that time.'

'But…' One glance at his face and I stop my protests. I sense a new tension in him. He's not often raised his hand to me, that was Ricardo's itch, but now his frustrations with his son and his health problems will be vented on me. I'll to have to watch my step, or things could get much worse. One word from Stefano and I'd be out on the streets. None of the other café owners would dare employ me if he did that. My heart thumps in my chest. I look down at the bowl of unpeeled potatoes and say, 'Yes, of course. Understood.'

In my head I'm reeling with fury at the injustice of it all. In this moment I hate this life and I hate Stefano too.

A day in Cardiff

'Don't fuss, Mamma, we're only going to Cardiff, not to the end of the world.' Olivia winks at me. We have the use of Sophia and Glyn's car today. A treat.

'But remember one time you run out of petrol. Is always good to check.'

I can see Olivia is desperate to get on the road and I'm looking forward to the trip as well. I've only been into Cardiff a few times and a day to visit one or two of the famous sites will give me some things to report to Mamma when I write next. She's still saying she misses me and carrying on with her advice, in every letter, for me to get in touch with Carlotta. 'Don't wait too long, *mio ragazzo*, or she'll get engaged to someone else.'

I'm startled from my thoughts by Signora Rossi pinching my cheek.

'Look at you two. What a handsome couple. I don't see why you not choose Angelo. Why you no see what I see – is a good man, hard worker, reliable and very handsome.'

Signora Rossi is only half joking and I feel guilty that my trip is built on a white lie. I do want to see the sights but the opportunity to spend time with Catherine again is the main attraction. And then, there's Olivia's mysterious boyfriend.

We head off, Olivia driving like a bat out of hell.

'Steady. We want to get there in one piece. And it's not your car.'

'But I promised Leon I'd be there by midday.' Despite the twists in the road we overtake several lorries and cars. Olivia means business. I wonder what this boyfriend is like. There must be something wrong with him if she doesn't want to tell Signora Rossi. I know from what she said before that he's not from Wales, and not Italian. But is there something else?

'I feel bad about your Mamma.'

'Sometimes it's the only way. She would like me to find a nice Italian boy, like you, but love doesn't work like that, does it?' Olivia has heard all about my Mamma's plans for me; and how I feel about them. 'Anyway, you've a golden opportunity to get to know

Catherine better by coming to Cardiff with me today, so don't you go complaining. I know you fancy her.'

The closer we get to Cardiff, the more nervous I feel. I don't belong in this city world with all the clever university students. And meeting Catherine again in that situation is terrifying. I try to explain to Olivia. 'What if she just sees me like a farm boy from Italy who can't speak proper English?' But Oliva is concentrating on getting us there as fast as possible and she's always had a no-nonsense attitude to problems.

We park the car in Cathays near her digs, a small terraced house in a row of similar streets. A gaggle of boys, around my age wearing striped scarves and Cardiff University sweatshirts, swarm around us and Olivia waves to a couple she knows. Then we're inside and, in the dark hall smelling of stale curry, I just manage not to catch my leg on the pedal of a bike leaning against the banisters.

'Go on through to the kitchen. I've got to get ready.' Olivia is already running upstairs to her room. 'Make yourself of a cup of tea or coffee.'

It's a long, galley kitchen with a door at the end looking out into the garden. A brighter room after the front part of the house, painted white and kitted out with a breakfast bar and stools. I decide to take Olivia at her word and make a cup of coffee. I'm bending in the fridge to find the milk when I hear Catherine's voice.

'Angelo. Great you were able to make it. 'Livia told me you were coming.'

And there she is, the girl of my dreams, her hair shining like spun gold, looking at me, so calm, slim and elegant.

'Oh, hello, Catherine.' Stupidly, I can't find any further English words. But she saves me.

'I've got a bit of preparation to do for school but then maybe if you'd like I'll show you some of the sights. We could go for a walk in Bute Park or something?'

The sun streams in through the window and soon we are talking, like last time, as though we've already known each other for years. Perhaps we did in another lifetime.

'Your English has improved by leaps and bounds.' I feel a glow of happiness that she sees how hard I am working on building a better life.

'Leaps and bounds?' I look at the curve of her cheek and her mouth.

'It's another of those idioms I told you about,' Olivia explains, rushing in to join us. She's a whirlwind today and stunning in a woollen maxi dress and boots. I don't know what she's done exactly, but her hair has been put up and she's wearing long earrings which make her look dramatic, more Italian. 'Means my boy's doing very well.' She pats me on the back.

The doorbell rings. She picks up her bag and coat. 'Be good. See you later.'

We're walking along the path by the River Taff. It's a warm, early autumn day. I'm so happy everything seems unreal, like in a dream. I'm sure a girl so beautiful must already have a boyfriend and she's just being kind. But that's enough for me.

'So, do you have any brothers and sisters?' she asks me and before long I'm telling her all about the farm, Mamma and why I left.

'You must miss it.'

'I went back this summer, first time for nearly two years.' I see her eyes widen in surprise. I suppose in her world that's unthinkable. 'It was good to see my mother and the family, but it was strange. I didn't feel like it was home anymore. I suppose I've changed.'

'I can understand that. Since I've been away at college, I look at my home in a different way.'

I wonder what she means. Her life must be filled with everything you could possibly want. Then I think, maybe that's the problem.

'It's difficult, but my mother, well, let's just say I wouldn't want her life. It's pointless. You know what I mean? Like a bird in a gilded cage. She's a trophy wife.'

'a trophy wife is. . .?'

'. . .the wife of a rich man with nothing to do except entertain her husband's business associates or do charity work.'

'This is a problem I've never seen.'

She laughs then. 'My sister has already rebelled. Dyed her hair, gone all hippyish, love and peace, man.'

Catherine does an impression of someone smoking a joint. 'Anyway, I'm going to make sure I get my teaching qualification so that I can be independent, use my brain.'

'I'm sure you will.'

‘Are you?’ Catherine turns to me, gives me her lovely smile. ‘That’s what I admired about you when we first met in Pontypridd. Your positive attitude.’

There’s a powerful silence between us. I would so like to take her hand, to hold her in my arms, but I’m frozen. I’m not worthy of such a girl, not yet.

‘Anyway, what’s this about Olivia’s boyfriend? Why isn’t she bringing him up to Ponty to meet her Mamma?’

‘I don’t think it’s a big deal, but then I don’t belong to the Italian Catholic community. I don’t think Mrs Rossi would approve.’

‘So, he’s not Catholic, or perhaps divorced? I had wondered.’

‘Yes…,’ Catherine hesitates, ‘Probably best if you keep this part to yourself – again I don’t think it’s a big deal – but he’s one of the tutors at uni. Doesn’t teach us. Livia met him when she was volunteering, or something.’

Now I know why Olivia doesn’t want to tell her Mamma. I feel uncomfortable that I’ve been used as cover today. I have a lot of respect for Signora Rossi, and I don't want to get in the middle of a nasty family mess. I'll have to speak to Olivia when I can.

I try to put my concern out of my mind as we go back to the house and Catherine entertains me by teaching me some English customs, explains these are different from Welsh ones. We're just on to Morris dancers, sitting opposite each other on the sofa and I'm laughing at the explanation she's giving, when the doorbell rings.

'That'll be Olivia I expect, forgotten her keys again. Being in love and all that.' Catherine runs down the hall and Olivia comes in, beams at me, grabs her keyring with a loco gesture to her temple and heads out to where the mysterious boyfriend is waiting. She sparks nervous energy and excitement.

'Pick you up in a couple of hours to get us back to Ponty.' She looks so happy. Maybe she is really in love. Maybe things will work out.

Catherine takes me to buy fish and chips and we eat them, relishing the chance to carrying on talking about her family and mine, about all our ideas for the future. I don't mention Mamma's marriage plans.

Meeting Catherine's parents

I'm feeling guilty as I've come to Cardiff with Olivia again, by train this time, on the pretext that I'm going shopping with her to find a new dress. The reality is different. Olivia has disappeared to be with her boyfriend. Signora Rossi knows nothing about him, of course. She thinks that Olivia and I are 'courting', as she puts it, and she's happy for us to go out together. She sees nothing strange in her daughter asking me to go to dress shops with her. If she only knew…As time goes on, I'm getting more and more worried about it all. She's bound to find out in the end.

In the student house where Olivia and Catherine live there are four girls sharing. Two of them seem to spend a lot of time with their boyfriends, although they're friendly enough when I've met them. They've got used to me, I suppose. There's a warm and friendly atmosphere, despite the cold and draughts, and the constant smell of fried food or curry. Sometimes when I'm here, I cook pasta for them. It's not proper stuff, dried, so Mamma and Signora Rossi would not approve, but with onions, garlic, herbs and tomatoes I make a sauce that they all love. Or pretend to. They tease me so much I'm never sure, but the food always disappears.

Everyone else is out today. Just Catherine and me. I like it. Despite our different backgrounds I feel comfortable with her. It's quiet here together. Only the buzz of distant traffic outside and the drum of the rain on the windows.

'Proper October,' Catherine says, 'What can we expect except rain?'

It's my third October in this strange land. Seems a lifetime. Things have changed. I've changed. I'm becoming used to the rhythms of the seasons and the customs of the people – just as I did at home.

Catherine is preparing for teaching practice and I'm given tasks to do; paper, scissors and a written sheet of instructions to follow. She thinks if I, with my improved, but still imperfect English, can follow her instructions, then her pupils should manage. They're nine years old. A cheeky laugh accompanies this comment. I frown and work out what's needed. I'm making a snowman shape and feel as pleased as any child when I finish with a flourish. Catherine laughs and then we're surprised by a knock on the front door. She answers and I can hear voices, mumbled at first and then clearer.

'Oh, it's you! What is a nice surprise! You didn't say you were going to be in Cardiff. Come on in.'

Catherine comes back, followed by a plump middle-aged man and a slim woman. She rolls her eyes at me in mock dismay before she gives the introductions.

'These are my parents, Angelo. Mum, Dad, Angelo. He's a friend of Olivia's. He's from Bardi, Italy.'

'Oh,' the woman looks at me and raises one perfectly formed eyebrow, 'and where is Olivia?'

I swallow, waiting. The way she speaks indicates, somehow, that to be Italian and here is wrong. I am in the wrong place, with the wrong girl. I wait, unsure if I should say anything. Catherine's mother is in her late forties perhaps, smart suit, high heels and a coat that's so well-cut it has to be very expensive. The man is the same. Shiny shoes and a trench coat buttoned over trousers with creases. He wears a hat and takes it off to reveal a head of greying hair, thin on the top. A few, chill raindrops land on my face. I make no move to get up from the floor where I'm sitting surrounded by bits of paper, scissors and glue. The snowman picture mocks me. Catherine doesn't hesitate, confident in herself, the situation.

'Olivia's gone to see her tutor. Some problem with her teaching practice, I think.'

I'm amazed at how easily the lie slips off Catherine's tongue. I thought she was always honest, but I suppose she can't really tell her parents that we suspect Olivia is having an affair with one of the tutors.

Catherine's father is staring at me. His nostrils flare a little and I can tell he doesn't like me. Working in the café has helped me read character quickly. I say nothing. There's a short silence as we weigh each other up; the parents and the boyfriend. Am I a boyfriend? I wonder about that. Olivia and I have flirted, but with Catherine it's different. I'm attracted to her but apart from brushing hands, or holding her while we danced that one time, we've not crossed the line between friendship and something deeper. I realise at that moment how much I long to be Catherine's boyfriend. To hold her close as we walk together; to kiss her; to be one half of her life.

‘I had a meeting in the city,’ her father’s voice is deep, gruff, commanding, ‘so your mother came too. We thought we could take you out for a meal. A surprise. We didn’t know you had company. I’m driving back home later.’

Catherine seems unperturbed by this, although my stomach is churning.

‘That sounds nice. I could do with a good meal, but I can’t really leave Angelo. I promised Olivia I’d look after him.’ Another lie.

‘Humph. Well, I suppose he’d better come too.’

Not the most gracious of invitations and I would prefer to stay here alone but already Catherine is on her feet, has handed me my coat and is halfway along the hall. What can I do?

Catherine and I get into the back of her father’s Mercedes and I feel sick with nerves. I’ve no idea what to say to these people. They speak in an accent like the Queen. Not at all like any of the people I’ve met since I’ve been in Wales. Thankfully, it’s only minutes until we arrive at the hotel car park and get out. It’s a luxury place in the centre of town. I’ve walked past it with Olivia but would never dream I’d enter it. I’m conscious of my faded jeans and shoes that have seen better days. I wonder if my coat smells of the café. Catherine links her arm in mine, smiles to give me courage as we follow her parents into the hotel.

It's not at all like Stefano's café. Here the tables are laid with starched white linen tablecloths. The lights shining on the silver cutlery and the sets of wine glasses dazzle me. The waiters move our chairs and unfurl the starched napkins with a flourish. My heart is beating loudly, I'm sure they can all hear it, and I feel so much out of my comfort zone I could be present at an interview with his Holiness, the Pope himself. Each place has an array of cutlery and at least three glasses. I widen my eyes in a silent plea to Catherine. What do I do?

The menu comes next. I'm handed what appears to be a large booklet with pages of writing. Some of it I recognise but when Mr Chadwick turns and says, 'So, Angelo, what are you studying?' my stomach does a flip and I think I'm going to be sick, there at the table. Then I feel Olivia's light touch on my arm and I turn towards her. Can she guess my panic? She gives me one of her sweet smiles and I try to breathe.

'Angelo's in catering. He wants to find out how the business works so that he can open his own restaurant. Italian food, of course. He's the most divine cook.'

Mrs Chadwick peers over the spectacles she's put on to peruse the menu. She has blue eyes, like Catherine's. 'Oh. And how have you sampled his cooking? When you went to stay with Olivia? Do you live in the sticks as well, Angelo?'

I frown. 'Sticks? No. We live in a proper house. Brick and slate roof. Olivia's Mamma, Signora Rossi, is my landlady.'

Catherine can't control a sudden fit of giggles. I see I've said something wrong again. Mrs Chadwick has the faintest ghost of a smile at the corner of her mouth, and coughs into her napkin to hide a laugh, but her husband just grunts. 'Better order now. What do you fancy?'

Once again, I'm stricken. Catherine points to something on the menu and says, 'I think I'll have the roast, please. No starter. Thank you.' She passes the menu to the waiter. Mrs Chadwick orders something that sounds fancy but turns out to be fish. I say, 'The roast, please,' and keep my fingers crossed.

We sit and talk. At least Catherine and her parents talk, and I try to follow. Her mother smiles at me now and again as if she understands my predicament. All the time I look towards the door and wonder if I could just get up and go. But the waiter has taken my coat and I'm not sure where it is. I feel so out of place. A stranger in a foreign place with people who are rich and more educated than me. I'm certain now that Catherine will never want me as a boyfriend. My heart is bruised by that thought.

The meal is pure agony and seems to last for hours. The food is wasted on me. I'm so nervous I have to force myself to swallow every bite. I drink water, although Mr Chadwick orders a bottle of wine. When at last it's over and we are able to leave, I stammer my thanks. Mrs Chadwick squeezes my hand and smiles. The rain has stopped and the sun's come out making everything look better. Catherine declines a lift back to the house.

'It's turned out a lovely day. I think we'll just walk back. Do a little detour through Bute Park. We've been stuck inside all morning.'

She gives her parents a peck on the cheek and they're gone. I can feel the tension leave my body. Catherine links her arm in mine.

'I'm sorry about that. Was it really awful? My parents are such snobs. But at least you got a decent meal and a look inside one of Cardiff's best hotels. You also stopped me from having the usual interrogation about what I'm going to do when the course is finished. Thank you.'

She leans close and gives me a kiss on the cheek. Her lips are soft. It's enchantment.

All the way back to Pontypridd I think of that kiss and what it could mean.

The telephone call

I'm awake before the alarm the next day. Catherine's faith in me and the short, but wonderful, time we have spent together has given me new energy and optimism. She can see something in me, and I'll prove her belief is right. I'll make a success of my new life. I walk on air through the chilly autumn streets, feeling as though I am making headway, beginning to find my place in this country. When I get to the café, I put the chairs down, the heating on and go into the back to take out a new bag of potatoes to peel.

'Good, that's good.' Stefano limps in, looking terrible. If he wasn't the owner, he should be off work. 'But don't think you can get away with anything, just because I'm unwell. Don't forget I know all about being tough. I was interned in the war.'

I've heard this story many times before and Signora Rossi has also talked to me about her husband's experiences. It seems unfair that if you've settled in a country and are working hard to pay your way, you should be seen as an alien. Makes me feel nervous. I'm clearly a foreigner, still not really fluent in English, although much improved. And the way Catherine's father looked at me, like a piece of dirt on his expensive shoe. He didn't see me as anything except an outsider, and a poor one at that.

I carry on peeling. By now I'm highly skilled at it and can think while I'm working. The radio is on in the background as usual, Radio One pop songs. John Denver's singing Annie's Song. Stefano likes that. Says the music makes me work harder. Well, he's the boss. I wonder what Mamma would think of him. I haven't told her everything about the way I've been treated because it would upset her. But she'd probably admire his business skills and the way he gets on with the customers. That reminds me to ask Signora Rossi whether she's put a letter aside for me from Mamma. Odd as I'm used to the weekly message, like clockwork. My thoughts are interrupted by the sound of Stefano's voice echoing from his office cubicle. I hear his side of the conversation. I guess he's talking to Ricardo.

'You can make good money here too.'

A silence, then Stefano's voice becomes more agitated. 'It's your duty. I've built this business for you, so you can take it over after me.'

There are unheard replies and finally the call ends. Stefano comes out. I can see fury and disappointment on his face. He doesn't say anything to me but later I hear him talking to the old guys, saying 'I've spoilt him, now he's too good to come back from London to Ponty, to waste his talents here. What a joke.' But it's obvious he doesn't think it's a joke.

I'm relieved at the news. Ricardo in Ponty is trouble for me; and probably Olivia.

For the next few weeks, I work twice as hard. Getting up in the dark and arriving home to Signora Rossi late in the evening. I don't get any thanks from Stefano. He sees it as his due. He's given me a chance. I owe him. I reckon after two years, though, I've more than paid my side of the bargain. I work as hard, or harder, than I used to work on the farm and in the last month I've more or less run the place. Stefano's been sitting, resting his bad leg, chatting to the customers and giving me orders while I've been working in the kitchen, serve, clean and wash up. Recently I've even done the books. Stefano's drinking more than he used to. He's left it all to me. Not sure if it's the alcohol or the pain in his leg. But I like taking charge. I've discovered I've got a natural way with looking at profit and loss; what we need to order; and trends in what the customers like. If I wasn't so exhausted, I'd see this new challenge as an opportunity.

'Stefano's not well, we all know that, but he needs get someone in to help until he's better.' Signora Rossi puts my pasta out one evening towards the end of October and, as usual, speaks her mind. 'You looking very tired. No point you get ill too. When you have last day off? You should have some free time, go to Cardiff with my Olivia.'

Signora Rossi is right. What with Stefano's illness and spurred on by meeting Catherine and her encouraging words, I'm working so hard I feel like a shadow. Sometimes I'm too tired to eat; sometimes I can't sleep thinking about what little chance I have to impress her or her parents. I wake up just before dawn one day from a nightmare where Mr and Mrs Chadwick are in the café, turning their noses up at the décor and sauce bottles.

'You talk to Stefano. Day off. Go out with my Olivia. She come to take me to Swansea, staying over next weekend. Try to get a day off.'

I nod, but I know it's hopeless. I need that time to catch up on the business side.

Olivia bounces in and chats to her Mamma about teaching practice and the children, telling a funny story about a little girl who's drawn a picture of her with Popeye because her mother told her about the cartoon character Olive Oyl. I haven't seen her for a few weeks, and I don't mean to get angry, but something about the way she laughs and jokes with Signora Rossi makes me mad. I'm working all the time. Work and sleep. No social life outside the café. No energy to do anything. What's the point? Olivia is much closer to Catherine than me. She speaks perfect English; she's clever and is going to be a teacher. When Signora Rossi goes into the kitchen to cook and we are sitting in the front room, my anger overflows.

'How's your boyfriend?'

She's not stupid. She can tell something's wrong. 'Okay.'

‘Or, should I say, tutor?’

Her face flames red and she looks towards the kitchen. ‘Ssh.’

The devil is in me. I can’t stop myself. I’m tired, fed up and frustrated. I need to take out my anger on someone. And she has it coming.

‘Because I don’t want to be the go-between any more. It’s not right. Your Mamma thinks we’re going out, that I’m your boyfriend.’ I’m so angry I’m almost stuttering. Thank God we’re speaking Italian because English words are not strong enough at this moment.

‘What’s got into you?’ I can see I’ve hurt her, but she’s angry as well.

‘I’m sick and tired of working all the hours and getting nowhere. And you…’

I throw a log into the fire. ‘You’ve got all this, a home, a future, education, the chance of a good job and… and still you have to go for one of your tutors.’

‘Shut up. Keep your mouth closed or you’ll be sorry.’ Her eyes lock onto mine, bright with fury. ‘Remember you’re only a lodger and I just have to say to Mamma you acted badly towards me and you’re gone.’

'Food is ready,' Signora Rossi's voice sings out. As Olivia leads the way into the kitchen, she hisses over her shoulder, 'Catherine says hi, by the way.' At the sound of her name, all the anger leaves me and I feel exhausted, deflated. How badly have I been behaving? I touch Olivia's arm.

'I'm sorry. I won't say anything.'

Olivia nods but her body is still tense. What a mess I've made of things.

By early November, I catch a bad cold, but I struggle on. Stefano is slowly getting better and has started taking over some of the work, complaining about the orders I've made and the way I've done the books. Still, we've made a profit. Anyone else would be grateful. He gives me my first day off for weeks and I go for a walk up Graigwen, which Olivia showed me when I first came to Ponty. I haven't seen her since we had our argument. Signora Rossi has noticed and asked what's the matter and why don't I go to Cardiff. I just say I'm tired with all the work. My temper outburst has only hurt me, as now Olivia isn't speaking to me and I don't have a chance to see Catherine. As I tramp up the hill, I tell myself it's for the best. It's hopeless anyway. Her parents have her future all mapped out, a rich banker like her father, so she can have the same sort of life she's always had. I go to bed early and for the first time in a long while, dream about the farm. One of the goats has caught its leg in the fence, Papa's blaming me, raising his hand. I wake up, sweating.

The next day I'm in the café clearing tables in a lull between customers when Stefano calls me over to his office. There's hardly room for the two of us in there, what with the table, chair, filing cabinet and shelves full of tins, bottles and wholesale stock. He's holding the phone out to me.

'Go on. It's for you.'

'Angelo?' Aunt Violetta's voice sounds distant and breathless. I imagine her in the telephone booth in La Pavane amongst all the telephone directories.

'Mamma. Is it Mamma?'

'She's been taken ill. Suddenly yesterday. You need to come. It's very serious.'

She tells me that Mamma collapsed yesterday evening and was rushed to hospital by ambulance. The doctors don't know what it is yet, but she's very ill. I can hardly believe it. She looked so much better when I saw her in September. I'd stopped worrying about her, seeing her settled and comfortable with Aunt Violetta.

I hand the phone back to Stefano in a daze. He's heard the whole conversation.

'Your mamma's very ill?'

I nod, staring at the rough hessian sack of potatoes in front of me.

'Well then,' he shifts on his bad leg. 'I'll get someone in to cover your work, maybe one of my cousins from up the valley, or one of the girls who come in for coffee.'

Stefano's kindness brings tears stinging to my eyes.

He pats me on the back. 'Go, just go straight away. We sons have to look after our Mammas.'

I set off that evening with a large parcel of food Signora Rossi gives me for the journey. As I wait in Cardiff station for the coach to London, a woman's voice calls out my name.

'Olivia!' Suddenly, out of the crowd, there she is, a familiar face. 'What are you doing here? Are you going to London too?' I'm stunned with the speed of events. Anything's possible.

'Mamma told me. I didn't want you to leave with all those bad words between us.' She throws her arms out and we hug. 'I'm so sorry about your Mamma and I hope she pulls through,' she whispers. 'She'll be happy you're with her. And Catherine sends her good wishes.'

I'm fighting tears again as I get on the bus.

'Look after yourself. Keep in touch,' she says.

As we pull out of the parking bay, I see her waving. Who knows when, or if, I'll be back?

Parma

Hospital

I come straight to the hospital when I arrive in Parma. The doctors decide Mamma needs to be here instead of Bardi. I've asked for information, but the nurses say little. At least she is alive. The doctor does his rounds in the morning and the afternoon sun is setting as I take a chair by Mamma's bed. That clinical smell of disinfectant mixed with food, and other things I prefer not to think about, assaults my senses. I've always hated hospitals. I had my appendix removed at thirteen and couldn't wait to get home again. Being here reminds me of the pain, the awful food and all the restrictions. No music, only two visitors and no wandering around. Not that Mamma is fit to get out of bed. She's lying, asleep, her breathing accompanied by a slight wheezing.

There are three other women in the ward. One's asleep, snoring, and the other two watch me with red, dry eyes. Curious about me, and why I'm here at this time, late evening. I've had to beg to be admitted, explaining how far I've travelled. I wonder if she's so ill they're afraid to deny me the right to be here. I know that the priest's been in. Aunt Violetta seems to think her condition is critical but still, I expect the nurses to ask me to leave at any minute. I listen to the loud tick of the clock.

When a nurse bustles in, all dressed in white, I look at her. She's young, about my age, with smiling eyes. She holds Mamma's wrist, takes her pulse while looking at a watch pinned to her uniform. If I want to know what's happening, I need to ask again.

'Is… is she going to be alright?' My voice cracks a little and I can feel tears threaten. I'm weary with travelling, light-headed, strung out like catgut with a confusing mixture of emotions.

Her eyes are full of sympathy. Despite the situation I can't help noticing how pretty she is. She regards me carefully before she speaks.

'Your Mamma is very ill. The next twenty-four hours will be the deciding point. She's calmed since you came. She knows you're here. Hold her hand, stroke it like this.' She demonstrates how to massage Mamma's hand using a little cream from a tube by the bedside.

I copy the movements and find it strangely comforting to be occupied instead of sitting staring at the crucifix on the wall. The nurse nods her approval.

'She's been given the last rites by the priest. She's in God's hands now.'

I gasp. Is this the end? Seeing my alarm, the nurse seeks to offer comfort.

'A precaution, but we know there is always hope and prayers. No-one can say for sure when a life will end. I've seen patients recover when it wasn't expected. Talk to her. She can hear you. Pray with her if you feel it will be a comfort.'

She smiles and leaves me there, gazing at Mamma. She's almost unrecognisable. Skeletal. Her eyes are sunken into the sockets, accentuated by black rings and her cheeks are hollowed out. Although her eyes are shut, I can see movements, like spiders dancing, under the lids. Pray? I have no words. What should I talk to her about? It's so difficult to know what to say but I make a tentative start.

'I've come to see you, Mamma. All the way from Wales. They told me you were ill, but I hope the doctors will be able to make you well again. You're such a strong person. I remember, when I was a small boy, watching you climbing the apple tree and wanting to be able to do the same. You used to dig the garden and work just as hard as Papa.'

Her fingers flutter in my hand so I carry on. 'I used to love it when you read to me as a boy. All those places we visited through stories. All the wonderful dreams I used to have.' I pause, waiting for something, anything to indicate she's listening. 'I'm getting used to life in Wales now. Stefano is pleased as I get on well with the customers. I wish you could see the café. It smells a little like Italy with the coffee machine in the corner but at the same time there's the fried food. Maybe next year, when you're better, you can come and visit. You'd like Signora Rossi and Olivia. Olivia's always laughing and smiling.'

I stop. I can't tell Mamma about Olivia's lover. What do I say next? I look around the ward. The woman in the corner is still asleep but the other two seem to be listening to me. I feel irritated at first, but I meet the eyes of the woman in the nearest bed to Mamma's and she nods and smiles at me. I think how boring to be stuck here in this room without any stimulus. The woman opens her mouth and says, '*Racconti una bella stori.*' Tell a beautiful story. It seems I'm providing entertainment for the ward. I carry on talking.

'Sometimes, when I go to Cardiff, I see Olivia's friend, Catherine. She's very beautiful. She would be described as an English rose. She's got long blonde hair and eyes as blue as the kingfisher's wing. I like her very much and I think she likes me.' The woman cackles at that and my thoughts wander to the day I left Cardiff. Was it really only two days ago? I can hear Olivia's words. 'Catherine sends best wishes.' What does that mean? My head is a jumble of thoughts and fears. My future hangs in the balance. What happens if Mamma dies? What about the debts? The farm? Stefano's café? Catherine? So much to think about that my head hurts.

The nurse comes back and takes Mamma's temperature. I look at her, questioning, but she just shrugs. '*Lo stesso.*' The same. '*Puoi continuare a parlare.*' Carry on talking.'

'Catherine's parents don't like me. At least, that's the impression I get. They're rich. Her father has hand-made shoes and her mother has long fingernails, painted pink. I don't think her Mamma does anything, although

Catherine says she does charity work. I'm not sure what that means. Catherine has a sister, Anne, who's younger and a bit of a rebel, I think. She dropped out of school and went travelling. I don't know where, but I expect her parents paid.'

I close my eyes and think how I should just like to sleep, here in this chair, but I keep on talking, telling Mamma, and the other patients, about how my life has changed since I left Italy.

'We went out to lunch in a big hotel near the castle in Cardiff. It was very *elegante.* We had white linen tablecloths and napkins. The menu was pages long and I didn't know what I should choose. I was so nervous the food tasted dry, and it was difficult to chew and swallow. We had wine too, although I drank water. Signor Chadwick is keen on wine and knows a lot about it. He travels to France often and visits vineyards. I tried to tell him about the beautiful Italian wines we have but he said he prefers French. I think it was his way of telling me he thought I was inferior.'

The woman in the bed next to Mamma makes a sound like a sneeze, but I see she's just tutting in response to my story. My mouth feels dry. Mamma's breathing seems to have slowed and taken on a more regular rhythm. I close my eyes. It seems I'm always in the wrong place. In Wales I still feel like an outsider, although many people who come to the café greet me with a smile. The Italian community there is very supportive too and we have good times when we meet, in between all the hard work. I'm not homesick in Wales now, but I still hate the weather, the cold and the rain.

And, here, in my home country, I also feel out of place. When I walk through Bardi, I don't feel I belong, like I used to. But where do I belong, I ask myself? What does the future hold? I think of an English girl with hair that smells as sweet as rosemary and skin so soft and smooth. I think of the land, the farm, and the feel of the clay beneath my fingers. Maybe I needed to go away to appreciate all that. I think of my landlady Signora Rossi, Olivia, Stefano and all those people in Pontypridd who nod and smile at me when I pass them on the street. I think of my uncle Carlo, Aunt Violetta; and Francesco who works so hard on the farm and makes it a success. If Mamma dies now, what should I do? I could sell the farm and set up my own café in Wales or I could stay in Bardi, find a wife and work on the farm. My head hurts with so much thinking and I sigh, long and loud. Maybe I could keep the farm if Francesco was happy to carry on running things and we shared the profits? It's all too much to weigh up.

I think I must have drifted into sleep but when I open my eyes again, although it's dark outside, it seems nothing has changed in the room. The crucifix still hangs on the wall. The air is still hushed. One woman still snores in the corner and the others doze too.

Mamma's eyes flicker and open, just for a moment. They seem to be glazed, unfocused. Is that a good sign or not?

'Mamma?'

I go to look for the nurse. Mamma is awake. My decisions about the future can wait for another day.

About The Author

J. L. Harland

J. L. Harland is the pen name we use when cowriting. It's a composite of our two names: Janet Laugharne and Jacqueline Harrett. We also write individually under our own names. In co-authored work we enjoy the buzz of sharing ideas and producing stories that have a unique, blended voice. J. L. Harland short stories have appeared in anthologies and online. Our debut novel is *'What Lies Between Them'*.

The novella, *'Angelo's Journey; From Bardi to Pontypridd'*, is the prequel to *'What Lies Between Them'*. Written in fictional memoir form, it is about Elin Fiorelli's father, Angelo and how, as a young man, a death in the family and debts forced him to leave Bardi, Italy and travel for work to Pontypridd Wales.

'What's Left Behind', due for publication in 2025, is the standalone sequel to *'What Lies Between Them'*. This novel tells how Elin Fiorelli's life takes a completely unexpected turn with the discovery of a letter found while clearing her family home.

Alongside a social media presence as JL Harland, we have presented our work at book fairs, libraries and various in-person events. We run workshops on our cowriting process and on writing in general. You can find out more about us at our web site– **jlharland.co.uk**

Individual writing

Janet Laugharne's debut poetry collection. *'Greenscapes... and other poems'* is available from her author page at erbacce-press and from local bookstores in Cardiff.

www.erbacce-press.co.uk/janet-laugharne

Jacqueline Harrett's crime fiction series features D. I. Mandy Wilde and is set in and around Cardiff. *'The*

Nesting Place', *'The Whispering Trees'* and *'With Grave Consequences'* are available from Amazon and Diamond Books.

harrett.co.uk

Books By This Author

What Lies Between Them

Elin Fiorelli, a career academic, has returned from three months in Finland to Brynderwen university, Wales. She thinks she has her future mapped out, a professorship within her grasp. But, her former lover, Michael Harwick, is now her boss. Her job is at risk and the ghosts of her past come back to haunt her with the secret she has kept buried deep within herself for so long. When her mother becomes terminally ill, trying to balance work and duty becomes more difficult. But Elin is resilient and as the year unfolds, she faces her past traumas, emerging stronger than before.

Book Club Questions

Angelo's Journey

1. This has been described as a coming-of-age story. Which aspect of his life do you think Angelo has found most difficult?

2. Do you empathise with Angelo?

3. Which character did you like the most? And the least? Why?

4. Did you have any empathy with Stefano?

5. Did the background to either place resonate with you? Do you remember Italy or Pontypridd in the 1970 or 80s? How have things changed in a place you remember from your younger days?

6. Angelo's physical journey from Bardi would have been long and arduous. How do you think travel abroad was different in the 1970s?

7. Angelo was an economic migrant, as many people are nowadays. What constraints on travel did Angelo have that still hold true for such travellers today?

8. With present day coffee shops emerging all the time do you see a parallel with the cafe culture of the 1970s?

9. Did any aspects of historical detail help you to understand Wales of the 1970s?

10. What do you think about Catherine's parents? Will Angelo ever be accepted by them?

11. The story is left at a crossroads. What do you think Angelo should do? Will it be Italy or Wales? Why?

Printed in Great Britain
by Amazon

45347517R00086